FERAL MAGIC

A GOODWIN

Disclaimer

This is a work of fiction. Names, characters, places, and incidents are products of the author's imagination or are used fictitiously. Any resemblance to actual persons, living or dead, events, or locales is entirely coincidental.

This novel contains themes of violence, transformation, grief, and emotional trauma, as well as references to blood magic and supernatural elements. Reader discretion is advised.

All rights reserved. No part of this publication may be reproduced, distributed, or transmitted in any form or by any means, including photocopying, recording, or other electronic or mechanical methods, without the prior written permission of the author, except in the case of brief quotations embodied in reviews or critical articles.

For the one who believed in monsters,

and in the girls who dared to love them anyway.

Thank you for the late-night talks, the quiet encouragement,

and the way you always knew where the heart of the story lived.

This one howls for you.

CHAPTER 1

Every curse begins as a prayer.

The forest was wrong. It always had been as long as she could remember.

The forest whispered around Grace as she moved cautiously through the underbrush, each step deliberate and careful to avoid the snapping of twigs. But the mist seemed to draw away from her, and the trees stood brittle and silent, as if unwilling to shield her. The early morning air was sharp, tinged with the earthy scent of damp moss and pine needles. Her breath clouded in front of her as she exhaled slowly, steadying herself. The dagger at her belt felt heavier than usual, a stark reminder of her duty — and the ancient weight the Hollow no longer wanted her to carry.

This was it. Her first solo hunt.

The Lutteux family had built its legacy on moments like these, where hunters stepped into the shadows of the Moonlit Forest to confront the darkness head-on. Her father's words from earlier that morning echoed in her mind: *"Stay focused. Trust your instincts. You're ready for this, Grace."*

But was she?

Grace paused at the edge of a small clearing, her gaze sweeping across the disturbed earth. Claw marks gouged deep into the bark of a nearby tree, and the grass was flattened, smeared with dark, rust-colored streaks that made her stomach churn. The scene was violent and chaotic, yet something about it felt... wrong.

Dropping to a crouch, she ran her fingers over the claw marks. They were jagged, deeper than she expected, but they didn't seem to match the calculated precision of a werewolf on the hunt. This wasn't the work of an animal stalking prey—it was desperation.

The mist shifted strangely as Grace moved deeper into the Hollow, coiling away from her boots, thinning as if the very ground refused her.
  She slowed, pulse hammering in her ears, when a flash of dark red caught her eye.

A blood trail — dark, drying already, weaving through the moss and dead leaves like a jagged wound.

The forest air thickened, sharp with the metallic stink of blood and something worse: fear.

Grace hesitated.

The dagger at her belt weighed her down like guilt.

The woods didn't want her here.

She could feel it now — the trees leaning away, the ground softening treacherously beneath her steps, the mist tightening behind her like a noose.

And yet she moved forward.

Each footprint she left was a betrayal the Hollow would remember.

A few paces in, she found a glove — torn, muddy, still damp inside. A few steps later, a leather satchel half-hidden in the ferns, its flap ripped clean off.

The blood was thicker here, pooled in irregular, frantic splashes.

Something had been chased.

Something desperate.

Grace's breath clouded in front of her, shallow and fast now. She tasted copper at the back of her throat.

Another broken branch. A gouge in the bark, deep and splintered — the desperate mark of a hand trying to flee.

She knew, even before she found the body, that she was too late.

He lay half-curled at the base of a gnarled tree, his clothes shredded, his face frozen in a grimace of terror.

The corpse had been savaged — torn open in brutal, inhuman rakes — and worse, left half-devoured.

Grace knelt, the cold seeping up through her knees, and pressed two fingers to what was left of his throat.

Still warm.

The hunter hadn't died long ago.

A fresh howl rose somewhere in the Hollow — not triumphant, but hungry.

The trees shivered with it.
   And Grace, for the first time in her life, realized she wasn't just unwelcome here.

She was prey.

A rustling sound snapped her attention to the treeline. Her heart leapt into her throat as she rose, her hand instinctively gripping the silver dagger at her belt. The forest fell unnaturally silent, the usual hum of life replaced by an oppressive stillness.

Her eyes darted between the shadows, searching for movement. The bracelet hidden beneath her sleeve began to warm slightly, a faint prickle against her skin that told her she wasn't alone.

And then she saw them—two glowing green eyes staring at her from the shadows.

But not the fevered, blood-red glow she'd been taught to fear.

These were clear — shockingly clear — a green so vivid it seemed to cut through the mist like a blade.

Grace's breath snagged in her throat.

The clearing seemed to contract around her, the mist thickening, the trees bending closer.

The figure stepped into the dim light, silent and smooth, like a predator that didn't need to rush the kill.

It wasn't a wolf, not fully.

It was a man — tall, lean, wild in a way no human could fake.

His dark hair fell in messy strands across his forehead, damp with mist. His hands hung loose at his sides, fingers slightly curled, like claws waiting for a reason.

But those eyes—

Not sickly, not corrupted.

Something clean. Something terribly alive.

And somehow, that made him even more frightening.

Grace reached instinctively for her dagger.

The man stilled, the barest tightening of his posture — not fear, but awareness, as if he were deciding whether she was worth the effort.

Her fingers fumbled the dagger hilt.

He took one slow step closer.

The ground seemed to ripple under her boots.

Grace braced herself, her heart battering her ribs hard enough she thought it might tear free.

"Who—" she began, but the word broke off into a whisper. Her throat was too dry, her body too slow.

The man — no, the werewolf, no matter what skin he wore — tilted his head, studying her with the unsettling curiosity of something that did not *have* to understand her to destroy her.

For a moment, the forest itself seemed to hush — no birds, no breath, just the two of them caught in a silence stretched thin as wire.

Move, her instincts screamed.

Run. Fight.

Do *something*.

But she couldn't move.

Because there was no immediate threat in his posture.

No snarl. No rush.

Just that calm, measuring stillness — the kind that came right before the kill.

And then his gaze flicked downward, lingering on her dagger.

His lips curved, slow and humorless, into something that might have been a smile — or a warning.

He lifted one hand — palm outward, fingers splayed, deliberate.

Not attacking.

Not surrendering.

Something in between.

"Not yet," he said.

The words slid across the clearing like mist — low, rough, and rich, edged with something that was not quite human.

Before Grace could react — before she could even breathe — he turned and melted back into the shadows without a sound, swallowed by the mist and the trees as if he had never been there at all.

Grace stood trembling, dagger raised uselessly, her breath clawing at her lungs.

The forest whispered again, but this time, she couldn't tell if it was warning her—

—or laughing.

Before Grace could process his words, he turned and vanished into the shadows, his movements impossibly quick. The forest seemed to exhale around her, the tension dissipating as birds resumed their songs in the distance.

Grace remained frozen, her grip on the dagger tightening as her mind raced. Who was he? And why hadn't he attacked her?

The warmth of her bracelet faded, leaving her with more questions than answers. She glanced back at the hunter, still dead at her feet and in the direction of the werewolf.

Not yet, what the hell did that mean?

Her first hunt was over, but instead of triumph, all she felt was confusion.

Clipping the dagger back onto her belt, Grace turned and began the trek back toward the Lutteux estate, her thoughts a storm of doubt and curiosity. The hunt had only just begun, and already, nothing was as it seemed.

The boutique lights buzzed faintly overhead, throwing sterile white across racks of glittering dresses.

Emily spun toward a rack of gold gowns, practically vibrating with excitement.

"This one!" she cried, yanking a dress free.
"Instant goddess. Come on, you'll melt hearts."

Grace managed a tight smile, folding her arms across her chest — conscious, suddenly, of how broad her shoulders felt under the harsh lights, how the curves of her hips strained the shape of her jacket.

She shifted her weight awkwardly, wishing for armor, not satin.

The hunter was dead.

And now here she was — pretending to be normal. Pretending to be a girl who cared about boys and dresses and fall dances.

"I don't think gold's really my thing," she muttered, voice rough with exhaustion she couldn't scrape away.

Emily rolled her eyes and grabbed another hanger — this time a slinky red thing that looked like it might vanish if she breathed wrong.

"You're too pale for pastels anyway," Emily said breezily. "You need something bold. Dangerous."

Grace let herself be shoved toward the changing rooms, the dresses draped over her arms — heavy as regrets.

In the mirror, she flinched.

The fluorescent lights were merciless —
highlighting every curve she hated, every line that felt wrong.

Her chest was too full for the sleek dresses Emily loved.
Her hips wide enough to tug the seams taut.
Her thighs pressed close when she stood straight.

Not sharp like the hunters were meant to be.

Not lean, fast, forgettable.

She pulled the red dress on first — and hated it immediately.

The cling of the fabric over her stomach.
The way it caught at her chest.
The way it shouted.

Too much.

The next dress was deep midnight blue.

Heavier fabric.
Smoother.
Richer.

It slid over her curves like water — not hiding them, but claiming them.

It made her look bigger, yes — broader, stronger — but it also made her look like something undeniable.

She stared at her reflection.

Not delicate.

Not perfect.

But powerful.

Heavy as a storm gathering on the horizon.

A dark queen in waiting.

For the first time in longer than she could remember, Grace didn't look away.

The dress whispered against the floor as she stepped out of the fitting room.

Emily's mouth dropped open.

"Oh my God," she breathed.

"You look like you're about to ruin someone's entire life."

Grace snorted softly, crossing her arms — feeling the heavy pull of the fabric, the weight of herself — and for once, not entirely flinching from it.

"If only it were that easy," she muttered.

Because she'd already seen what she was going to ruin.

Not boys.

Not hearts.

Fates.

The green-eyed stranger waited in the edges of her mind — still and patient, a shadow stitched into the fabric of her world now.

Emily didn't notice the shiver that chased down Grace's spine.

She just twirled her finger in the air.

"Spin, dummy. You have to see how it moves!"

Grace gave a slow, reluctant turn.

The dress flared around her like midnight unfurling — regal and ominous.

She chose the midnight dress.

Because deep down, she knew ruin was already written into her skin.

The Lutteux estate loomed like a stone sentinel against the fading twilight, its ancient spires casting long shadows over the grounds. Grace paused at the gate, her fingers curling around the cold iron. She inhaled deeply, steadying herself for the questions—and judgment—that awaited her inside.

The sound of her boots on the cobblestones seemed louder in the stillness of the evening as she approached the heavy oak doors. They groaned in protest as she pushed them open, stepping into the dimly lit foyer. The weight of the house pressed down on her, the air thick with unspoken rules and the echoes of her ancestors.

Her father was waiting in the study.

"Grace." John Lutteux's voice carried a sharp edge, as if he had been rehearsing his disapproval since she left that morning. He stood behind the massive oak desk, a ledger open in front of him, though it was clear he wasn't reading it. His piercing gaze locked onto her, dissecting her with a single glance.

"You're back earlier than I expected," he said, his tone carefully measured. "What did you find?"

Grace hesitated, the image of the man with green eyes flashing in her mind. She had spent the walk back rehearsing what she would say, but now, standing before her father's unyielding presence, the words felt tangled and fragile.

"There were signs of a struggle," she began, keeping her voice steady. "Claw marks, blood—but the scene didn't make sense. It wasn't... typical werewolf behavior."

Her father's jaw tightened. "Did you see it?"

"Yes."

"And?"

Grace faltered. She could still feel the warmth of her bracelet, and hear the man's calm, enigmatic voice. Not yet. What was she supposed to say? That the werewolf hadn't attacked her? That it had walked away, leaving her unharmed?

"It escaped," she admitted, the weight of the words settling heavily between them.

The silence that followed was suffocating. John's hand came down hard on the desk, the sharp crack echoing in the room.

"Escaped?" he repeated, his voice low and dangerous. "Do you have any idea what you've done? A werewolf doesn't just escape, Grace. You had one job—one opportunity to prove that you're ready to carry this family's legacy—and you failed."

Grace flinched but forced herself to meet his gaze. "It wasn't like that," she said, her voice firmer than she expected. "Something was off. This wasn't a rogue werewolf hunting for prey—it was different. I think—"

"I don't want your theories," he snapped, cutting her off. "I want results. The people of this town depend on us, and you've jeopardized their safety with your hesitation."

"John."

The soft voice broke through the tension like a gentle breeze. Marielle Lutteux stepped into the study, her calm presence immediately grounding the room. Her dark hair was pulled into a simple braid, and her hands were clasped lightly in front of her, but there was a quiet strength in her posture.

"That's enough," she said, her gaze steady as she looked at her husband. "Grace is safe, and that's what matters."

John's lips pressed into a thin line, but he didn't argue. Instead, he turned his attention back to the ledger, dismissing Grace with a wave of his hand. "We'll talk more about this later. For now, go."

Grace didn't need to be told twice. She turned and left the study, her shoulders tense as she made her way down the hall.

"Grace," her mother's voice called gently.

She paused, turning to see Marielle standing in the doorway, her expression soft with concern.

"You did well," Marielle said, stepping closer. "Trust your instincts, even when others doubt you. They'll guide you better than any rule ever could."

Grace's chest tightened at her mother's words, the quiet reassurance cutting through the disappointment that weighed heavily on her.

"Thanks, Mom," she said, her voice barely above a whisper.

Marielle smiled, brushing a strand of hair from Grace's face. "Get some rest. Tomorrow is another day."

Grace nodded, retreating to the sanctuary of her room. The moonlight spilled through the window, casting shadows on the walls as she sank onto her bed. Her father's words still rang in her ears, but so did the memory of the werewolf's eyes—calm, knowing, and entirely unlike anything she had been taught to expect.

Her instincts were telling her something, and for the first time, she wondered if her family's legacy had been built on a foundation of half-truths and blind tradition.

The hunt was far from over, but Grace knew one thing for certain—her path would not be dictated by fear or expectation.

It would be her own.

CHAPTER 2

The trees rose tall and ash-white, their branches bare and trembling as if whispering secrets to a moon that pulsed like an open wound above. Everything shimmered—not with light, but with tension, as though the dream itself was holding its breath.

Grace stood barefoot in a clearing flooded with silver mist, her hands empty, her heart racing. Before her, a wolf knelt.

Not crouched. Not snarling. *Knelt.*

Its black fur was matted with blood, streaked with silver like veins of moonlight carved into flesh. The creature's chest rose and fell in ragged bursts, breath steaming against the cold that wasn't cold. Around its neck hung a broken charm—twisted silver and garnet, glinting like something familiar. Its eyes, when they met hers, were not feral.

They were *mourning*.

The ground beneath her bare feet was slick — sticky — *warm.*

She staggered, glancing down.

Blood.

Dark and gleaming, it clung to her skin, seeping between her toes, painting her pale flesh with a violence that felt both foreign and inevitable.

A tremor tore through her, but she didn't pull away.

Instead, something surged up inside her — sudden, searing, unstoppable — like fire shattering ice, like lightning lashing a frozen sea to life.

Power.

Sorrow.

Bound together in a knot so tight she could hardly breathe.

She should have been afraid.

She should have wept, recoiled, fled back into the empty safety of the woods.

But she didn't.

She stood in the blood, feeling it soak into her skin, claiming her.

And in that terrible, echoing silence, she understood:

This was no accident.

She had been chosen.
 Not saved.
 Not spared.

Crowned in silence.
 Anointed in blood.

The wolf bowed its head to her, and something ancient in her blood *thrummed*.

A voice, warm and womanly, rose behind her.

"You're doing well, child."

Grace turned, but there was no one there—only a shadow behind the trees, long and graceful and gone before she could blink.

The forest cracked like breaking bones.

Grace woke with a gasp, heart hammering against her ribs like it was trying to escape. The room was still dark, her bedsheets twisted around her legs, the bracelet on her wrist burning cold.

She lay back slowly, staring at the ceiling.

She didn't know what the dream meant. But she knew it wasn't just a dream.

Not anymore.

The sharp, earthy tang of pine filled the air as Grace Lutteux perched on the window seat in her room, the moonlight spilling in like liquid silver. Her fingers brushed the worn leather of her mother's old hunting journal, its cracked spine whispering secrets of battles fought in the shadows. Yet, her mind wasn't on the inked pages in her lap—it was far away, in the heart of the forest on a night she could never forget.

She was eight years old again, breath held tight in her chest, crouched low behind the gnarled roots of an ancient oak. The woods were hushed but expectant, as if the trees themselves were listening. Her fingers, small and scraped, dug into the rough bark, anchoring her to the moment. Above, the moon was fat and cold—watchful.

Her brother Virgil had taken the Silver Oath that morning, the ceremonial blade pressed to his palm as he vowed to protect the bloodline. Thirteen and trembling with pride, he had looked at their father as if waiting to be made into something more than a boy. Grace had not been allowed to come, of course. "Too young," her father had barked. "Too soft," her mother had said, though without cruelty—just the truth of a woman who had seen too much.

But she had followed anyway.

The forest had always called to her—not just the thrill of danger, but something older, more intimate. She had slipped from her bed and tracked their bootprints through the mud, all the way to the clearing where the first hunt was meant to begin. Where her brother would prove his worth.

That was the night she saw it.

The wolf emerged from the shadows like a wound torn into the world. Massive. Silent. Its fur was a shifting black, darker than shadow, and its eyes—its eyes were not red with rage, nor wild with the madness her father had described. They were *clear*. Not human. But not lost.

She should have screamed.

Instead, she stared.

Then it saw her.

The wolf stilled, its breath steaming in the cold air. It tilted its head—curious, not murderous. No growl. No snap of teeth. Just that gaze, steady and almost sorrowful, fixed on her like it recognized her. Like it mourned her.

She didn't move.

Then came the crack of a branch. Her father's call. The silver light of a drawn blade.

The wolf lunged—not for her, but toward the sound.

And then Virgil was there.

He threw himself between them, shouting her name as the wolf struck. She would never forget the wet, awful sound of claws meeting flesh. The way Virgil hit the ground. The blood that bloomed bright against the silver-threaded cloak he had worn for the first time that morning.

The wolf recoiled at the sight of the boy it had wounded. Snarling, backing away—not attacking again, not finishing it. Its body trembled, as if caught between instinct and memory. Then it turned and vanished into the night.

Her father's fury came swift. His shame, sharper still. But it was Virgil's silence—his clenched jaw, his averted eyes—that haunted her.

What Grace remembered most wasn't the pain or the punishment. It was the moment before the wolf turned. The flicker of something almost human in its gaze.

Not a monster.

Not yet.

Now, years later, Grace couldn't shake the memory. It was more than just a moment of childhood rebellion—it was a fracture in the narrative she had been taught. Monsters were dangerous. Monsters had to be destroyed. But that wolf... it hadn't been a monster, had it?

Grace closed her mother's journal and looked out at the forest beyond the Lutteux estate. The trees stood tall and dark, a fortress of secrets waiting to be unveiled. The wolf's eyes, so full of pain and defiance, lingered in her mind, a haunting reminder of a truth she couldn't deny.

Monsters, she thought, tracing the edge of her silver dagger with trembling fingers, **were not always what they seemed.**

The stories told by firelight said the cursed howled only for blood. That under the full moon they lost all reason, tearing flesh from bone, leaving nothing but ruin in their wake. And it was true—partly. The transformation came with the moon's rise, wrenching bone and mind alike. First came the hunger. Then the rage. And last, the forgetting. Language eroded. Memory bled away. Eventually, there was nothing left but the beast.

But it wasn't the bite that doomed you. That was the part most got wrong.

The curse didn't pass with teeth—it passed with blood.

That lesson had been drilled into her long before she made the vow. A cut shared in battle. A wound tended too slowly. Blood mingled, and that was enough. A single heartbeat of vulnerability. That was all it took to begin the unraveling.

She could still hear her uncle's voice from training: *"It's not about the wounds you see—it's about the blood you don't notice until it's too late."*

She looked down at her wrist.

The charm bracelet gleamed there—delicate silver links catching moonlight, deceptively innocent. Each charm marked a piece of her family's legacy: a tiny wolf's tooth, a hunter's arrow, a drop of garnet like spilled blood. Her mother had fastened it herself just days ago, with hands that shook more than Grace had expected.

Seventeen. Years older than Virgil had been. Her family had waited, doubted, hoped she might never have to take the oath. That maybe she would choose a quieter life. But Grace had made her vow anyway. Whispered it beneath the Hunter's Moon with the forest watching.

The bracelet had burned cold against her skin ever since.

She was a hunter now.

But the creature she'd seen that night behind the oak tree—the one with sorrow in its eyes—still haunted her.

Because it hadn't looked like a monster.

It looked like a warning.

CHAPTER 3

The crisp morning air bit at Grace's skin as she stepped onto the training grounds behind the Lutteux estate. Dew clung to the grass, sparkling under the pale light of dawn. The quiet of the early hour was broken only by the rhythmic clink of steel as Virgil sharpened a blade on the whetstone. The steady motion of his hands was precise, mechanical, and full of the tension that had become a constant in their interactions.

"About time you showed up," Virgil said without looking up. His voice carried a sharp edge, as if the act of sharpening his weapon extended to his words. "Father told me to run drills with you. Not that you're ready for anything serious."

Grace bristled at the jab but swallowed her retort. She hadn't slept—*not really*—the unsettling dream still clinging to her skin like cold sweat. Her father's disappointment hung over her like a storm cloud ready to break. And almost tripping over her aunt's pug that morning—its small body slinking across her path like a shadow—had sealed her fate. She could still feel its wet nose brushing her ankle, the faint snort of laughter following her out the door.

"I'm here, aren't I?" she said, her tone defensive as she crossed her arms.

Virgil set the blade aside and rose to his feet, towering over her with a presence that was more intimidating than his actual stature. His dark hair was tied back, and the scar running from his jaw to his collarbone caught the light, a constant reminder of the injury he never let her forget.

"Let's see if you can do more than just 'show up,'" he said, tossing her a wooden practice sword. Grace caught it awkwardly, the rough wood stinging her palms.

"Let's see if you're finally worth the blood we've wasted on you," he said.

Grace gritted her teeth.

They squared off in the circle — Virgil braced, weight forward like a man already planning to hurt.

Grace's stance was careful, knees bent, heart hammering.

She knew better than to expect a fair fight.

"Come on," Virgil taunted.

"Or are you planning to *hesitate* again?"

The words slammed into her gut.

She charged without thinking — a wild, reckless swing toward his shoulder.

He blocked easily.

Too easily.

His wooden blade smashed against hers with a jolt that rattled her bones.

The shock drove her back a step — but she caught herself, breath hissing out between her teeth.

"You're slow," he snapped.

"And soft."

He came at her — three blows in rapid succession.

One slammed her ribs.

One clipped her thigh.

The third — a brutal, backhanded swing — **caught her jaw.**

The crack of it echoed in the frozen air.

Grace reeled, the world tilting sharply.

Stars burst behind her eyes.

The taste of blood flooded her mouth.

She stumbled — barely keeping her feet — clutching the wooden sword like it could anchor her.

Pain throbbed instantly across her face — sharp, hot, blooming out from the hinge of her jaw.

Virgil didn't apologize.

Didn't hesitate.

He advanced again — practice blade raised — like he meant to finish it, to put her on the ground and leave her there.

Grace staggered back, lifting her own blade in weak defense — she was off-balance, dazed, not fast enough.

"Virgil."

Marielle's voice, slicing through the cold.

He hesitated — just for a breath — blade freezing mid-swing.

"Drop it," Marielle said again.

No scream.

Just steel.

Virgil's eyes flicked from Grace's bruised, bloodied face to Marielle's unmoving figure.

Something twisted deep in him.
 Something ugly.

But he obeyed — tossing the practice sword aside like it disgusted him.

Without a word, he turned and stalked away toward the manor, boots crunching hard against the frozen ground.

Grace stood frozen, her chest heaving as she fought to hold back tears. Marielle approached, her expression softening as she placed a hand on Grace's shoulder.

"You're stronger than he gives you credit for," Marielle said gently. "And you'll prove it. Not to him, but to yourself."

Grace nodded, though her heart still ached. She gripped the practice sword tightly, staring at the scuffed wood as if it held the answers she needed. Her jaw throbbed with each beat of her heart. The forest loomed in the distance, a reminder of the battles yet to come.

And for the first time, Grace wondered if she would ever truly be ready.

CHAPTER 4

Grace tugged at the hem of her jacket wishing it were bigger, lower, covering her curves, as she walked up the steps to Blackwood High School, her stomach churning with unease. The familiar red brick building loomed ahead, its arched windows glowing faintly in the morning light. She could already hear the buzz of students inside—laughter, conversations, the occasional slam of a locker.

She didn't want to be here. After the failed hunt and her brother's cutting words, the thought of facing her classmates felt like stepping into another battlefield. Worse still, she'd have to face *them*—Jenna Taylor and her pack of sharp-tongued followers, who always seemed to find new ways to needle at Grace's insecurities.

She adjusted her bag on her shoulder and tried to shrink into herself as she stepped inside. The hallway was a chaotic river of bodies, but Grace weaved through it with practiced efficiency, keeping her head down and avoiding eye contact. She barely had time to reach her locker when a familiar voice rang out behind her.

"Well, look who decided to grace us with her presence," came a saccharine-sweet voice that made Grace's stomach drop.

Jenna Taylor was leaning against a nearby locker, her entourage flanking her like the guards to a queen. Jenna's perfectly styled hair shimmered under the fluorescent lights, and her painted lips curled into a smirk as her eyes scanned Grace with thinly veiled disdain.

"Still rocking the oversized look, huh?" Jenna said, loud enough for the surrounding students to hear. "I mean, I get it. It's not like *your size* is easy to shop for."

The laughter that followed was sharp and cruel, slicing through Grace's already frazzled nerves. She kept her eyes on her locker, fumbling with the combination as her hands shook.

"Careful, Jenna," one of her cronies said, feigning innocence. "She might snap and sit on you."

Jenna burst out laughing. "Good point. Maybe I should back up a little, just to be safe."

Grace's face burned, and her jaw clenched as she fought to hold back tears. She wanted to say something—anything—but her throat felt tight, the words caught in a knot of shame and frustration.

"Hey, Grace," Jenna continued, her tone mockingly sweet. "You should really join the fall festival this year. I hear they're looking for volunteers for the livestock tent. I mean, you'd fit right in."

Another round of laughter echoed through the hallway, but before Grace could muster a response, the bell rang, signaling the start of the next period. The sudden burst of activity broke the tension as students began to scatter to their classes.

"Saved by the bell," Jenna muttered, rolling her eyes as she turned to her friends. "See you around, *Gracie.*"

Grace exhaled shakily as the group moved away, their laughter fading into the din of the hallway.

"Grace!" a familiar voice called, and she turned to see Emily hurrying toward her, her blonde curls bouncing with every step.

"Are you okay?" Emily asked, her face etched with concern, her eyes on the bruise no makeup could fully hide..

"I'm fine," Grace lied, forcing a tight smile. "It's just Jenna being Jenna."

Emily frowned, placing a hand on Grace's arm. "You know you don't have to take that crap, right? She's just a sad little tyrant with no personality beyond making people feel small."

Grace appreciated Emily's unwavering support, but the words didn't make the sting go away. She shrugged and turned back to her locker, focusing on retrieving her books. "Let's just get to class."

She adjusted her bag on her shoulder and tried to shrink into herself as she stepped inside. The hallway was a chaotic river of bodies, but Grace weaved through it with practiced efficiency, keeping her head down and avoiding eye contact.

"You won't believe it!" Emily said, practically bouncing on her toes. "We have a new student today! And he's hot. Like, movie star hot."

Grace raised an eyebrow. "And you've already scoped him out?"

"Duh," Emily said, flipping her hair dramatically. "It's my civic duty as a friendly classmate to welcome the new guy. Plus, he's in our English class, so you'll get to see him soon enough."

Grace chuckled, shaking her head as she stuffed her notebook into her bag. Emily's relentless enthusiasm was a welcome distraction from the weight pressing on her.

"Seriously, though," Emily said, lowering her voice conspiratorially as they began walking toward their first class. "You have to check him out. He's got these piercing green eyes—like, stare-into-your-soul green. It's almost creepy, but in a really hot way."

Something in Emily's description made Grace falter. Green eyes. The memory of the man in the woods flashed through her mind—the way his gaze had seemed to see straight through her, his enigmatic words lingering like a shadow.

Grace opened her mouth to respond, but Emily wasn't finished.

"Oh—and speaking of creepy," she added, voice dropping even lower, "did you hear about that guy they found? The one out by Lutteux Hollow?"

Grace's stomach tightened. "What guy?"

"A land developer or something. My dad said he'd been arguing with the county over expanding into the old woods. They found his body two nights ago." Emily shivered, her grin slipping into something smaller. "No hands. No tongue. And his head was, like, clean off. Some people are saying animal attacks, but..."

She trailed off, waiting for Grace to fill in the blanks.

Grace didn't. She just nodded, face unreadable, heart suddenly thudding against her ribs.

The woods didn't give back what they took.

"Grace? Helloooo?" Emily waved a hand in front of her face, pulling her back to the present.

"Sorry," Grace said quickly, shaking off the thought. "I was just... distracted."

Emily gave her a knowing look. "You've been distracted a lot lately. What's going on?"

Grace hesitated, the weight of everything she couldn't tell Emily pressing down on her. "Nothing. Just tired, I guess."

Emily frowned but didn't press further. "Well, maybe the new guy will perk you up. I mean, who doesn't love a little eye candy to brighten their day?"

CHAPTER 5

They entered the English classroom, and Grace spotted him instantly.

Back row. Relaxed posture. A kind of stillness that didn't belong here — not in this flimsy, fluorescent-lit room where everything was supposed to be *safe*.

He shouldn't have been here.

He shouldn't have been anywhere near her.

Dark hair, messy like he'd run his hands through it one too many times.

Sharp, angular features — a mouth that looked carved for sin, not for smiles.

And those eyes.

Green.

Piercing.

Alive in a way nothing human should be.

Not corrupted red like the monsters she hunted.

Not dull with human blindness either.

Clear. Alive. *Watching.*

Their gazes locked — just for a second.

The world *stilled.*

Her heart dropped like a stone.

Under her sleeve, her bracelet pulsed with heat. A warning.

A silent scream.

"That's him," Emily whispered, bumping her elbow into Grace's ribs. "Told you. *Total hottie.*"

Grace couldn't answer.

Couldn't breathe.

Because this wasn't some hot new boy.

This was a threat.

And worse — he was everything she wasn't supposed to want.

Grace tore her gaze away, the movement jagged, stuffing herself into a desk near the middle of the room. Emily prattled on beside her about the Fall Festival, about caramel apples and cider, but it barely registered.

The air was wrong.

The space around her felt *wrong*.

Tight. Electric. Watchful.

Grace slid her notebook out mechanically, but her eyes kept pulling back to him — against her will, against her training.

He was flipping through a battered copy of *Wuthering Heights* like he belonged there, like he wasn't a wolf draped in secondhand denim.

Like he hadn't looked at her like he already knew the weight of her blood.

She should have wanted to run.

She should have wanted to slit his throat.

Instead, she wanted to tear open the space between them.

To close it.

To touch the heat she could feel radiating from him across the room.

God, she hated herself for it.

She almost heard her father's voice: *Assess the threat. Plan your action. Act.*

But all she could do was sit there, burning and frozen at once, while the bracelet at her wrist burned hotter — *not enough to stop her, just enough to remind her she'd been warned.*

The bell rang.

The lesson dragged on like wet wool, every tick of the clock a slow unspooling of her nerves.

She didn't dare turn around.

Didn't dare *look*.

But she *felt* him.

Static brushing the fine hairs at the back of her neck.

Heat blooming low in her stomach — fear and something darker she didn't dare name.

Other girls noticed him too — Grace saw it from the corner of her eye.

A dropped pencil. A loud, bright laugh.

The ways they twisted toward him like flowers straining for sun.

He ignored them all.

But Grace?

Grace felt *watched*.

Not admired.

Not flirted with.

Studied.

Owned.

She gripped her pen so hard the plastic creaked in protest.

The bell finally clanged again, signaling the end of class. Chairs scraped. Backpacks zipped. Voices blurred.

Grace lingered.

She didn't know why.

She told herself it was just to pack up slowly. Just to breathe.

Not because she wanted him to speak to her.

Not because a terrible, traitorous part of her wanted to hear her name on his lips.

The classroom emptied around her.

Emily was halfway out the door, tossing a "hurry up" glance over her shoulder.

Grace bent to retrieve her bag — deliberately slow, buying seconds.

And when she straightened, he was standing there.
Leaning against a desk.
Watching her.

"Grace Lutteux," he said.

Her heart nearly stopped.

His voice was *everything it shouldn't be*:
Smooth. Deep.
A velvet knife against her throat.

"How do you know my name?" she demanded, the words brittle, cracking at the edges.

A smile tugged at the corner of his mouth.
Small. Unreadable. Dangerous.

"Everyone knows your name," he said lazily. "The Lutteux are legends around here."

Grace crossed her arms, fists hidden, knuckles white.
Trying to seem normal. Unbothered.
Trying and *failing*.

"Yeah, well," she said. "Legends are mostly lies."

"Maybe."
He tilted his head slightly, studying her.
A man who already knew the shape of her scars.

"But there's usually some truth buried under the blood."

Grace's mouth was dry.
She hated how badly she wanted to step back.
How badly she wanted to step closer.

"Who are you?" she asked.

"Lucas," he said simply.

"And what do you want?"

Lucas smiled — a real smile, and it ruined her — sharp and feral and beautiful.

"I want your help."

Grace blinked. Confused. Angry.
 Hungry.

"My help with what?"

He pushed off the desk, slow and deliberate.
 Closed a fraction of the distance between them.

The bracelet at her wrist scalded her.
 She ignored it.

"I know what your family does," he said, voice dropping lower.

"I know what you're supposed to be."

His eyes flicked to the bracelet — not scared, not different — just *knowing*.

"And I know," he added softly, "you're not like them."

Grace's blood roared in her ears.

"You don't know anything about me."

"Don't I?"

His gaze pinned her.

Green and pure and utterly merciless.

"You hesitate. You wonder. You ache. You don't just see monsters."

His words cracked something inside her she didn't even know was brittle.

"I don't want your flattery," she snarled, stepping back.

Lucas only shrugged, almost lazy. Almost bored.

"This isn't flattery, Grace," he said. "It's recognition."

Before she could answer, he moved — a single step back — and the spell snapped.

He was at the door, one hand on the frame, looking over his shoulder at her like she was something inevitable.

"Old clearing. After school," he said. "Come if you want the truth."

Then he was gone.

Leaving Grace standing alone in the wreckage of her own wanting.

"See? Told you," Emily said, grinning. "And he couldn't stop looking at you, girl. He's *all yours.*"

Grace spun to face her, sharper than she meant to. "He's dangerous. Promise me you'll stay away from him."

Emily blinked, then laughed, tossing her hair over her shoulder. "Jeez, Grace, he's already yours. Chill."

"I'm serious," Grace snapped. The urgency in her voice cracked something raw. "Stay away from him. You don't know what he is."

Emily raised her hands in mock surrender, still grinning. "Yeah, yeah. Some *killer* smile he's got, though."

Grace stared at her, heart hammering, realizing just how alone she really was.

CHAPTER 6

The sun sagged toward the horizon, staining the sky in bruised golds and dying reds as Grace crossed the school parking lot, her bag slung over one shoulder.

The crisp autumn air nipped at her cheeks, sharp with the scent of fallen leaves and cold exhaust. She felt sick with nerves, caught between dread and something darker she didn't dare name.

She hadn't seen Lucas since English.

Part of her was relieved.

The other part — the part she hated, the part she couldn't scrape clean — kept replaying the way his eyes had pinned her. The way his voice had wrapped around her name like it belonged there.

He knew things.

Things he shouldn't.

Grace paused at the edge of the field, the normal world blurring into background noise.

Laughter, shouts, the clatter of cleats on pavement — none of it mattered.

Because there he was.

Leaning casually against the bleachers.

Hands shoved into his jacket pockets.

Wind tousling his dark hair.

Watching.

Not openly.

Not aggressively.

But with the quiet, unbearable patience of a predator who already knew you would come to him.

Her stomach twisted violently.

He shouldn't have looked so human.

So easy to want.

From here, he looked like every bad decision a girl could make — all lazy grace and sharp smiles, the kind of trouble you ran toward even as you swore you weren't running at all.

The bracelet on her wrist ignited.

Not warmth this time — *heat.* Sharp and brutal. A warning brand.

Grace stumbled back a step, sucking in a breath through her teeth.

It hurt. It wanted to be obeyed.

But her feet refused to move.

Because Lucas's eyes — green, bright, impossibly alive — had found hers.

And he didn't look away.

The smirk was gone.

There was only a terrible, aching stillness in him now, as if the boy everyone else saw had been stripped away.

Her instincts howled.

Run. Draw the dagger. Strike first.

Instead, she stood there like a fool, the bag slipping from her shoulder, the blood hammering at her temples.

Every training lecture, every warning her father had drilled into her mind snapped uselessly apart.

He was the thing she was supposed to hunt.

The monster.

So why did he feel like something her body remembered?

Why did part of her want to step closer — to see if he smelled the way she imagined — dark earth and rain and the dangerous edge of something wild?

God, she was broken.

The bracelet's heat pulsed, frantic. Begging her.

She ignored it.

Lucas moved first.

He pushed off the bleachers with that same terrible ease — every line of his body promising violence or salvation, depending on which side you ended up on.

But he didn't come toward her.

He only stood there, hands loose, head tilted slightly as if he were... *listening.*

Waiting.

For her.

Grace's hands clenched uselessly at her sides.

She wanted to shout at him, curse him, *cut him down where he stood.*

She wanted to close the distance between them until she could press a hand to the pulse in his throat and feel whether it beat like hers.

Weak. Broken.

When he finally turned — a slow, deliberate pivot — and disappeared into the tree line, she gasped like she'd been held underwater and only now allowed to breathe.

The bracelet cooled abruptly.

Too late.

Grace dragged it from under her sleeve.

The metal left a raw red welt across her wrist, the shape of the runes biting into her skin.

Still trembling, she whispered his name.

"Lucas."

Fear. Fascination. Fury.

All twisted together until she couldn't tell where one ended and the next began.

He wasn't just another monster.

He wasn't a boy.

He wasn't even a mistake.

He was temptation itself — the kind that left you marked even when you managed to walk away.

And Grace wasn't sure she could.

The forest swallowed sound as Grace entered the clearing.

Silver moonlight bled down through the trees, turning the earth to bone dust beneath her boots.

The dagger was already in her hand, hidden inside her

sleeve but ready — a sliver of cold resolve in her sweating palm.

She was not coming unarmed.

She was not coming blind.

Lucas waited in the center of the clearing.

No weapon.

No armor.

Just him — tall, loose-limbed, the night hanging from his shoulders like a cloak.

When she stepped into view, he lifted his hands — palms open, a show of peace.

But it fooled no one.

Grace's grip tightened instinctively.

The weight of the dagger was comforting.

A lie she clung to like a drowning girl.

"Grace," he said — and somehow, in the empty hush of the clearing, it sounded like both a promise and a dirge.

She kept her distance, heart hammering, tracking the space between them with the precision her father had drilled into her:

Ten feet.

Enough time to draw.

Enough time to react.

Enough time to kill — if she was lucky.

But even as she measured, she knew.

It wasn't enough.

Not against him.

Not against something born for speed and violence.

If he chose —

If he wanted —

She wouldn't even have time to scream.

And from the flicker in his eyes — the quiet sorrow, the brutal patience — he knew it too.

"You came," Lucas said, voice roughened by something she couldn't name.

Grace shifted her stance, letting the dagger flash half out of hiding — enough for him to see the silvered threat glint.

He only lowered his hands slowly, like a man accepting a truth he could no longer fight.

"I won't hurt you," he said quietly.

Grace almost laughed.

Could hurt her.

Would break her without even meaning to.

Lucas took a careful step forward —

And then he saw it.

Her jaw.

The ugly, blossoming bruise purpling her pale skin, stark against the silver light.

His entire body stilled — every muscle gone rigid, every line of him coiled tight as wire.

His eyes darkened — not with hunger, not with calculation — but with something far more dangerous:

Anger.

Not at her.

For her.

Before she could react, he moved — fast — so fast the dagger barely twitched from her hand before he was there.

Not grabbing.
 Not striking.

Brushing.

With terrifying gentleness, he reached out, the backs of his fingers ghosting up to touch her throat — her bruised jaw — so lightly she might have imagined it.

The dagger clattered to the ground between them, forgotten.

His fingers trembled once against her skin.

A breath shuddered through him — a guttural sound, half a growl, half something broken and human.

He was furious.

Not at her.

At whoever had *marked her.*

And for one terrible second, Grace thought — *he's going to lose it.*

Not on her.

For her.

Lucas realized it too — and jerked his hand back like he'd been burned.

He stepped back.

Two paces.

Three.

Wide enough to give her air.

Wide enough to let her pretend she had never been vulnerable at all.

But the space meant nothing.

Because if he chose — if he wanted —
He could cross it again.

Faster than breath.
Faster than fear.

To help.
To harm.

And they both knew it.

Grace stared at him, her heart hammering in her ears.
Not just from fear.
Not anymore.

Lucas's hands dropped loosely to his sides.

His voice, when it came, was wrecked and low.

"Who did that to you?"

Grace swallowed hard.

The answer stuck in her throat like splinters.

She wanted to lie.

To laugh it off.

To deny it meant anything.

Because if she told him —

If she gave him that truth —

He might not walk away from this clearing without blood on his hands.

Instead, she said nothing.

The dagger lay in the dirt between them, forgotten.

For the first time, she didn't feel like she needed it.

Not because she was safe.

Because she wasn't.

Because she was *seen*.

And God help her, part of her didn't want to run.

She bent and picked it up anyway, holding it tightly. They both knew he let her. She ignored the question, he gave her that too.

Would destroy her if he wished — that was the real truth sitting unspoken between them.

She edged a half-step back.

Not running.

Not surrendering.

Just... trying to give herself the illusion of space.

Lucas watched her — not cruel, not cold.

Just *aware.*

Predator awareness.

She might have the dagger.

But he had the power.

If this went wrong — it wouldn't be a fight.

It would be an ending.

And somewhere beneath her fear, beneath the thrumming ache of survival, another feeling coiled tighter:

Want.

Not for safety.

Not for mercy.

For him.

The real him.

 The dangerous, unknowable thing standing quiet and patient and inevitable beneath the broken moon.

"You said you had something to show me," she said, forcing her voice to stay even.

Lucas nodded.

"Not here," he said. His gaze brushed over her dagger, and something almost like sadness flickered across his face. "It's not safe."

"You're not safe," she snapped, the words sharper than the blade she carried.

A faint smile, hollow as a cracked bone, tugged at his mouth.

"No," he agreed.

 "I'm not."

He turned then — not in retreat, not in fear.

Just... waiting.

Trusting she would follow.

Knowing she already had.

Grace clenched the dagger tighter, the metal biting into her palm.

If she followed, she was stepping past the last barrier.

No hunter.

No monster.

Just her — a girl walking toward a boy who could kill her without a sound if he chose.

And somehow, she wanted it.

Wanted to know if he would.

Wanted to know if he wouldn't.

She moved.

One step.

Then another.

Across the distance she had tried so desperately to keep.

Into the reach of something wild and doomed and **beautiful**.

The dagger stayed in her hand.

A useless prayer against the inevitable.

The clearing faded behind them.

And Grace stepped willingly into the dark.

Not prey.

Not a predator.

Something else entirely.

Something *becoming*.

The deeper they went, the darker the forest became.

Moonlight bled away, strangled by the grasping trees.

The path narrowed until they walked in single file, Lucas leading, Grace trailing — dagger still clutched against her ribs like a secret.

The cold bit harder here.

The air smelled sharper — blood and damp earth and something older.

Grace kept three paces behind him.

Close enough to see him, far enough to draw the blade across his spine if she had to.

If that would even matter.

Lucas slowed near a crooked elm and waited for her to catch up.

When she drew level with him, he didn't move.

Didn't speak for a moment.

The silence stretched so thin it hurt.

Finally, he said, voice low and hoarse, "You know the stories, don't you?"

Grace tightened her grip on the dagger.

"About the curse?"

Lucas nodded, slow, like every motion cost him.

"Blood-bound. Passed through generations. Transformation under the full moon."

He recited it like a prayer — or a eulogy.

"But that's not the whole truth."

Grace stayed rigid, watching him out of the corner of her eye.

His body radiated heat in the freezing air.

It drew her like a moth to a dying flame — stupid, inevitable.

"And what is?" she demanded.

Lucas turned to face her fully.

His green eyes caught what little light there was — no red, no rot — just something raw and *aching*.

"The curse is changing," he said. "Twisting. Corrupting. It's not about rage anymore."

He paused, searching her face — searching for what, she didn't know.

"It's about hunger."

Grace swallowed hard.

The woods felt closer now, pressing against her skin.

"What kind of hunger?"

Lucas's mouth curved, not a smile.

Something sadder.

Something so much worse.

"The kind you can't starve out," he said. "The kind that wants more than blood."

His voice was almost a whisper.

And the way he looked at her then — like she was the only thing left that mattered — made her stomach knot and her thighs clench and her lungs *burn*.

Grace took a stumbling step back.

Lucas didn't follow.

He just stood there, hands loose, offering no threat.

Letting her see what he could be if he chose.

"If you stay," he said, "you need to understand."

"Understand what?"

"Those monsters don't just kill you," Lucas said quietly.

"They pull you apart first.

They make you want it."

The words hit her like a blow.

Because some part of her already knew.

Some desperate, broken thing inside her already *wanted* him — the real him, the dangerous him — wanted to lean in, not away.

Grace shoved the thought down.

Forced herself to focus on the facts.

"Who's doing this?" she asked, voice rougher than she wanted.

Lucas hesitated.

"A witch," he said finally.

"Someone who knows the old blood magic. Someone who's twisting it. Binding wolves to hunger instead of the moon."

His hand twitched — a small, unconscious motion toward her.

He stopped himself before he touched her.

But the damage was done.

Her skin ached for the contact that never came.

"And you?" Grace asked, stepping just far enough back to pretend she wasn't already inside the trap.

"You're just... what? A warning?"

Lucas exhaled sharply, something between a laugh and a sigh.

"I'm proof," he said.

"Proof that it's too late for some of us."

Their eyes locked — and in that raw, frozen moment, there were no lies left between them.

He could kill her.

She could kill him.

Neither wanted to.

Not yet.

Grace's dagger hung limp in her hand now, useless, forgotten.

She hated him for making her hesitate.

She hated herself more.

"You should have stayed away from me," she said, the words barely more than a breath.

Lucas's throat worked as he swallowed.

"Maybe," he said.

A half-step closer.

"But you didn't want me to."

The cold pressed closer, but Grace didn't move.

Lucas watched her like he was memorizing the shape of her hesitation — the way she clutched the dagger but didn't lift it.

A beat passed.
Then another.

It was Lucas who looked away first.

"Selene," he said quietly, the name like a stone dropped into a deep well.

"My sister."

Grace swallowed, throat dry.

"You said she was cursed," she managed.

Lucas nodded.

The tightness in his jaw returned — the effort of *not* breaking.

"We were born into it," he said. "The bloodline. The burden. We learned how to survive it. How to chain it."

He glanced at her again, eyes hollow.

"But we weren't prepared for what came after."

"What happened?" Grace asked, voice low, careful — as if the forest itself might shatter if she spoke too loudly.

Lucas exhaled, a slow, broken thing.

"There's... something old stirring beneath the curse. Something deeper than blood. It found Selene first."

He rubbed a hand over his mouth, the motion raw with frustration.

"She didn't just shift anymore. She lost herself. Piece by piece."

He pressed two fingers lightly to his temple, then to his heart.

"Gone. Not the way wolves lose control under the moon — this was different. This was permanent."

Grace shivered.

"How do you know it wasn't just the curse?"

Lucas's laugh was low and empty.

"Because she came back once," he said. "Just for a minute."

He stared into the trees as if he could see it playing out still — the memory eating him alive.

"I found her after a full moon. Blood everywhere. Three hunters dead. She was crouched in the mud, crying. Tearing at her own skin like she could claw the wrongness out."

His voice cracked on the last word.

"I tried to reach her. I called her name. She looked at me — and for a second, it was her. My sister. My best friend."

He shook his head, slow and broken.

"And then she changed again.
 Something *else* smiled out of her mouth."

The silence strangled the clearing.

Grace could barely breathe for it.

She thought of all the monsters she had hunted, all the things she had killed without hesitation.

None of them had been loved like this.

None of them had been missed.

"Why are you telling me this?" she whispered.

Lucas finally met her gaze — no shields now, no games.

"Because if you help me find her..."

He took a half step closer, enough that Grace could smell the salt-and-iron sharpness of him, alive and real and wrong.

"...you need to understand."

His voice dropped to a whisper.

"I'll do anything to save her.

But if she's gone — if all that's left is the hunger —"

His hand flexed loosely at his side.

"I'll kill her myself."

Grace staggered a step back.

Not from fear.

From the crushing weight of it — the terrible, beautiful loyalty inside him.

He wasn't a monster because he could kill.

He was a monster because he *could love something broken enough to kill it himself.*

"You shouldn't trust me," Lucas said.

Not a warning.

Not a threat.

Just the truth.

"You should have run the second you saw me."

Grace's dagger was still in her hand.

Her training screamed that she was already too close, already too lost.

But she didn't move.

Because part of her — the part she couldn't scrub clean no matter how hard she tried — understood him.

Understood what it meant to love something you couldn't save.

To hate yourself for trying anyway.

She slid the dagger back into her jacket.

Slow. Deliberate.

Lucas watched the motion, a flicker of pain crossing his face, so fast she almost missed it.

"Where do we start?" she asked, voice hoarse.

The relief that washed across Lucas's features made her chest ache.

"Tomorrow," he said.

"I'll show you."

The clearing breathed again around them.

But Grace knew the air would never taste clean here again.

Not after tonight.

Not after him.

"Okay," she said at last, her voice steady. "Show me... But if you betray me, Lucas, I won't hesitate to finish what my family started."

A flicker of relief passed across his face, but he didn't smile. "Fair enough."

As the moonlight bathed the clearing in silver, Grace felt the weight of her decision settle over her. She had crossed a line tonight, one she couldn't uncross.

And she had no idea where this path would lead.

The woods were thick with mist when Grace realized she was not alone.

It started as a feeling—a prickle at the back of her neck, the tightening of the air.

The kind of tension that only came when something was watching.

She slowed her steps, hand going to her dagger. The silver bracelet on her wrist thrummed cold and fast, vibrating against her skin in frantic pulses.

A shadow flickered between the trees.

Grace turned in a slow circle, heart hammering against her ribs.

"Lucas?" she called out, voice too thin in the heavy mist.

Silence.

Only the wet sigh of the wind through the skeletal trees.

Another flicker of movement—closer now.

The bracelet flashed cold again, warning.

Her stomach twisted.

No. No, not him.

But a shape moved in the mist—tall, broad-shouldered, predatory—and something deep inside Grace clenched.

Betrayal bit harder than fear.

Her chest hollowed out with the terrible realization: *he must have lured her here.*

He must have never meant it—the kisses, the promises, the slow breaking of her walls.

A stupid, naive girl.

A hunter too soft to survive her own curse.

She cursed herself under her breath, drawing her dagger in a tight, white-knuckled grip.

You should have known. You should have known.

The figure crept closer, silent, relentless.

"Lucas," she spat into the mist, voice cracking. "Coward."

Her bracelet flared again, almost burning.

Something lunged.

Grace barely had time to twist aside as the figure burst from the mist—a blur of rage and claws and tangled hair.

Not Lucas.

A woman.

Small, sharp-boned, wild-eyed—striking with the precision of a predator.

Grace hit the ground hard, the breath knocked from her lungs as they rolled, locked in a desperate fight.

The woman clawed at her, snarling, eyes fever-bright and rimmed with red.

Grace fought back, adrenaline crashing through her, mind reeling.

Not Lucas.

But who—?

They separated, panting, crouched in mirrored stances.

The woman's lips peeled back from her teeth in a snarl.

And then, with a shudder, she forced out a single, broken word:

"Lucas."

Grace froze.

The woman lifted her head—and Grace saw her eyes.

Green.

Achingly, gut-twistingly familiar.

Grace's dagger slipped a fraction lower.

"Selene," she whispered, the betrayal bleeding out of her in a flood of horror and sorrow.

It had never been Lucas.

It had never been betrayal.

It had only ever been grief.

Selene crouched low again, muscles trembling—not attacking now, but still wild, still wary.

Grace straightened, lowering her blade slowly.

"I'm not here to hurt you," she said, voice rough, ragged. "Or him."

They stood locked like that—two broken creatures tangled in a war neither had asked for—until Selene, with a shuddering breath, backed into the mist and was gone.

Leaving Grace alone with her shame.

And the unbearable relief that she hadn't lost him—

yet.

CHAPTER 7

The room was wrong.

Grace stood in the center of her mother's workroom, though it looked more like a forgotten chapel—its beams warped, the stained-glass windows leaking red light instead of color. The butcher's table gleamed beneath flickering candlelight, though she didn't remember lighting any. The air stank of copper and burnt herbs.

She was barefoot.

And the pug was there.

It sat near the corner, eyes glinting like twin coals, snorting wetly with each breath. It padded toward the table, tongue lolling. Something dark dripped from the edge of the butcher's slab—*thick, red, and still warm.* The pug licked it eagerly, snuffling, its small body trembling with excitement.

Grace's stomach twisted.

A silver bowl sat on the floor, filled with dark red thread. Wet. Tangled. *Breathing.*

She turned—her mother stood behind her.

But not quite.

Marielle's eyes were shadowed, her mouth stained like she'd bitten into something rotten. She didn't speak at first—just watched the pug licking the blood, her expression unreadable.

Then:

"Blood remembers. Even when we don't."

Grace opened her mouth to ask what that meant—but her voice caught in her throat.

"You think she chose you, Grace?" Marielle's voice was soft now. Too soft. "She didn't. She *made* you."

The red thread slithered across the floor like a trail of veins, coiling toward her bare feet. Grace stumbled back, heart thudding, but her boots were gone. She was rooted. Caught.

The pug looked up from its feast, muzzle soaked.

It grinned.

Grace woke with a snarl caught behind her teeth.

Her head throbbed, her arms ached, and her mouth still tasted like blood and thread. The dream clung to her skin like oil, slick and unwelcome. Her mother's voice echoed in her ears—*Blood remembers.* The pug's grin flashed behind her eyes.

And worse: the promise she'd made. To walk into the dark. With *him*.

She couldn't sit with it.

So she didn't.

She found Virgil in the training yard, just as the early morning frost still glittered on the stone. He was alone, running drills—silver-blade flashes and breath clouds, each movement precise, practiced.

Grace stormed across the yard without a word.

He looked up. Paused.

"What's that face?" he said. "Nightmares?"

"Fight me."

He blinked, then scoffed. "Seriously?"

"Fight me."

She didn't wait for his answer—she lunged.

He parried out of instinct, stepping back with a scowl. "Grace—"

"You've been treating me like a trainee for years," she snapped. "I'm done."

Their blades clashed, steel singing sharp and fast. Grace moved harder than usual—less measured, more desperate. Virgil deflected, countered, pushed.

"Still sloppy," he muttered. "Still leading with anger."

"Still acting like a sanctified bastard," she spat, catching his wrist and twisting, but he rolled free.

The sparring turned mean.

Not training.

Not even a test.

Just rage.

Virgil pressed her back with a shoulder slam that nearly knocked the wind from her. "This isn't going to fix whatever nightmare you dragged in with you."

"You think this is about a *dream*?" she snarled. "You've looked down on me since the day I picked up a blade."

"I *trained* you," he growled, pressing in harder. "I *protected* you."

"I never asked you to!"

That made him falter.

Just a second.

Enough.

She dropped low, rolled under his guard, and used her elbow—not her blade—to catch his ribs and send him crashing to the ground.

Both of them froze.

Virgil stared up at her, breathless, stunned.

Grace stood over him, panting, sweat slicking her brow, dagger trembling in her grip.

Then he laughed. Not unkindly.

"Well, damn," he muttered. "She finally woke up."

Grace didn't smile. Didn't say thank you. She sheathed her dagger and turned away.

But for the first time in years, Virgil didn't call her back.

The lunchroom hummed with the usual chaos of clattering trays and overlapping conversations. Grace sat at her usual corner table with Emily, picking at her salad while her best friend launched into an enthusiastic recap of the latest school gossip. Despite Emily's chatter, Grace's mind was elsewhere—still circling the cryptic encounter with Lucas earlier that morning.

"...and then I said, 'No way,' because seriously, who even *wears* paisley anymore?" Emily said, pausing mid-story when her eyes flicked toward the room's entrance. "Oh, great. Here comes trouble."

Grace followed Emily's gaze and groaned inwardly. Jenna Taylor strutted into the cafeteria, her perfectly coiffed hair bouncing with every step. As always, she was flanked by her loyal entourage, their laughter echoing like a pack of hyenas.

Grace ducked her head, hoping Jenna wouldn't notice her, but the effort was futile. Like a shark scenting blood in the water, Jenna zeroed in on her immediately.

"Well, if it isn't *Gracie Lutteux*," Jenna drawled, sauntering over with a smirk. "Still trying to hide behind your little salad, huh? Adorable."

Emily stiffened beside Grace, but Grace raised her head and met Jenna's gaze. "Hi, Jenna. Shouldn't you be off terrorizing someone else? I hear the debate team could use a punching bag."

Jenna's smirk faltered for a fraction of a second before she recovered. "Oh, don't flatter yourself. I just thought I'd check in and make sure you're doing okay. You know, with all that... extra baggage you're carrying." She made a pointed glance at Grace's figure, eliciting giggles from her entourage.

Emily opened her mouth to fire back, but Grace held up a hand, silencing her friend. "Extra baggage? Oh, you must mean my brain. Yeah, it's heavy carrying around all this intelligence. You'd know all about that, right, Jenna?"

The laughter from Jenna's friends faltered, and one of them awkwardly coughed.

Jenna's eyes narrowed, her voice losing its syrupy edge. "Funny. You're a lot braver when you've got your little sidekick around."

Grace leaned back in her chair, a faint smile tugging at her lips. "And you're a lot less scary when you're trying this hard. What's the matter, Jenna? Run out of original insults?"

Emily snorted, unable to hold back a laugh. The sound seemed to send Jenna over the edge.

"You think this is funny?" Jenna snapped, her face flushing with anger. "You don't belong here, Grace. You're just—"

"Just what?" Grace cut her off, standing up so quickly her chair scraped against the floor. She locked eyes with Jenna, her voice steady and cool. "Say it, Jenna. Whatever pathetic little insult you've got lined up next, just spit it out. Or better yet, save us both the time and go find someone else to bother. You're boring me."

The cafeteria went quiet, dozens of heads turning to watch the confrontation. For a moment, Jenna seemed at a loss, her mouth opening and closing like a fish out of water.

Grace didn't wait for a response. She grabbed her tray, shot Emily a reassuring smile, and walked away, her steps firm and confident.

Behind her, the murmurs of surprise and laughter spread through the room like wildfire.

"Wow," Emily said, catching up to Grace in the hallway. "That was... amazing. Where did *that* come from?"

Grace shrugged, though her heart was still racing. "I guess I'm just done letting her walk all over me."

Emily grinned. "Well, I'm officially impressed. Remind me never to get on your bad side."

Grace laughed softly, but the victory felt bittersweet. It wasn't just Jenna she was standing up to—it was the voice in her head that had spent years telling her she wasn't enough.

And for the first time, Grace felt like maybe—just maybe—she was ready to prove that voice wrong.

Grace sat on the edge of the courtyard wall, boots resting on the frost-dusted stone, her fingers absently tracing the knots in her red thread bracelet. The sun was beginning to slip behind the trees, gold leaking into gray.

Emily dropped into place beside her, breath clouding the air.

They didn't speak at first.

Grace didn't need to say anything. Her silence was loud enough.

Emily finally broke it.

"You've been weird lately."

Grace smirked faintly. "Thanks."

"I mean it." Emily glanced at her, eyes sharp beneath her bangs. "You're pulling away. You flinch when I touch your arm. You look at the forest like it's talking to you. And you've been—" she hesitated "—*thinking* things. Dangerous things."

Grace's fingers stilled.

Emily continued, voice low and careful now. "I know something's happening. And I'm not asking you to tell me everything. I know that's not how this works. But if you're going to do something—*something irreversible*—I need to know you've thought it through."

Grace turned to her, throat tight. "What makes you think I'd do anything like that?"

Emily gave a dry laugh. "Because I've known you since we were eight, and you only get this quiet when you're about to leap off something high."

Grace looked down at her hands.

"I just..." she swallowed. "I don't know what's right anymore. I thought I did. I thought I was supposed to follow orders, carry the blade, and protect the town. But what if I'm not supposed to protect them the way they told me?"

Emily was quiet for a moment. Then she said, gently:

"Just be sure, Grace. Be *sure* of where you're going before you take too many steps to turn around. Because there's some roads—some choices—you don't come back from."

Grace didn't answer right away.

She just nodded once, slowly.

And when Emily left, Grace stayed behind.

The sun dipped lower.

And in her pocket, her fingers curled around the folded scrap of paper she hadn't yet written.

CHAPTER 8

The trees whispered as the sun dipped low, their bare branches clawing at the dusk. Grace stood at the edge of the forest, heart drumming a slow, steady rhythm beneath her ribs. The dagger at her hip was familiar—worn silver hilt shaped to her palm. The one in her boot? Sharper. Lighter. Unseen.

She had come prepared.

She always did.

Her red thread bracelet was knotted tight against her pulse, thrumming like it *knew* something she didn't. A charm woven from bloodline and whispered warnings—Marielle's voice echoing in her mind: *"It only works if you believe in it."*

Grace didn't believe in much anymore.

Lucas stood in the shadows just beyond the treeline, leaning casually against a birch as if he weren't a question she hadn't yet dared to answer. His dark hair caught the last golden light, his white shirt clinging to him like a secret.

Pretty as sin. Tasty as chocolate. And just as likely to kill you if you weren't careful.

He smiled when he saw her. Slow. Crooked. Dangerous.

"You came."

"I said I would."

"You're armed."

"I said I'm not stupid."

He laughed—quiet, warm, and absolutely unreadable. "Fair."

Grace didn't step forward. Not yet. Her fingers brushed the vial at her belt—a small glass cylinder wrapped in leather. It held a sedative strong enough to knock out a half-turned wolf for ten minutes. Not long. But enough.

And before she left campus, she'd slipped a letter through the slats of Emily's locker. Just a single line written in her sharpest hand:

If I don't show up for first period, ask my mother where the red thread leads.

Emily wouldn't find it until morning.

Her family would rage. But they'd know what to do.

If it came to it.

"Where are we going?" she asked.

Lucas turned, beckoning into the woods. "Somewhere old."

"Are you planning to kill me there?"

His lips twitched. "Not tonight."

That wasn't a no.

She stepped forward, every breath heavier now, every footfall deliberate. The forest seemed to exhale as she crossed the threshold, branches shifting above her like watchers leaning in.

"I'm trusting you," she said quietly, drawing level with him.

Lucas glanced down at her wrist, at the red thread glinting like a wound.

"No," he said, voice low. "You're preparing for me."

She didn't deny it.

For a moment, the space between them buzzed—charged with something unspoken and old. Her silver bracelet was cool against her wrist, not cold. Not warning her.

Lucas held out a hand. Not touching. Just offering.

"Trust me," he said. "Just for tonight."

Grace stared at him, her heart pounding hard enough to echo in her ears.

Then, slowly, she stepped forward and followed him into the woods.

Every step deeper felt like a question she didn't know the answer to.
But his shadow was steady ahead of her.
And sometimes, she thought, the only way to survive the darkness was to walk straight into it.

The air in the abandoned pack den was heavy with pain and silence, broken only by the faint rustling of leaves outside. Grace stood in the center of the largest shelter, her eyes sweeping across the room. The etched wards on the walls shimmered faintly in the dim light, their intricate lines a testament to the powerful magic that had once protected this place.

"How long has it been empty?" she asked, her voice quiet.

"Months," Lucas replied, his tone low. He leaned against the entrance, his sharp green eyes scanning the forest beyond. "After the corruption spread, those who weren't affected scattered. The ones who stayed..." He trailed off, his jaw tightening.

"Didn't make it," Grace finished for him, her voice tinged with unease.

Lucas didn't respond, but his silence spoke volumes. Grace felt a pang of guilt, knowing her family had likely contributed to the den's desolation. For generations, the Lutteux name had been synonymous with the eradication of werewolves, but this place was a stark reminder that not all of them were the monsters her family believed.

Lucas stood with his back to her, shoulders rigid, as if the weight of memory alone might crush him if he dared turn around. The forest around them was still, breathless. A hush like mourning threaded between the trees.

"She was the Howlkeeper," he said finally, voice low, frayed at the edges. "Selene. My sister. She kept the stories. The songs. She remembered every name, every vow. She led the moon binding rites when our alpha died."

Grace remained silent, her breath catching on the cold air. She didn't move closer.

"She wasn't supposed to be part of the hunt," he went on. "But she said the pack needed more than teeth. That someone had to protect the *meaning* of it all." His hands curled at his sides, not fists exactly—just the tense, trembling shape of someone trying not to break. "Now she barely remembers her own name."

The silence pulsed between them, thick with things not said.

"She trembles," he said, finally turning slightly, just enough for Grace to glimpse the pain shadowing his face. "Even in human form. Her eyes—when the moon touches her—they burn red like fire caught behind glass. And there's this... pulse. You can *feel* it. Like the forest goes wrong around her. Like magic wants to flee."

He looked down, jaw clenched.

"That's how you know. When the curse has gone too far. When corruption sets in."

Grace's fingers brushed the edge of her silver bracelet, suddenly cold against her wrist. The stories she'd grown up with didn't prepare her for this. For the aching absence of what had been lost.

"She used to sing the bindings in the old tongue," Lucas said, barely a whisper now. "Now she screams at the moon."

He turned his face away again, his voice flat and final.

"There are no rites left. Just ruins."

Grace didn't speak. Couldn't. The silence between them stretched long and aching, filled with truths she didn't want to hold. She watched Lucas—how he stood as if braced against a storm that had already passed but left him hollowed out.

Executioners.

The word echoed in her chest like a bell struck too hard.

That's what the Lutteux were, weren't they? Not guardians. Not saviors. Her ancestors hadn't sung healing rites or offered mercy. They had wielded silver and fire. They had named themselves righteous and called it duty. But duty had sharp edges, and hers had always come with a sheath.

She thought of the Hall of Names, of polished weapons laid beneath portraits, of whispered prayers soaked in blood. Every story she'd grown up with was lacquered in glory. But Lucas's voice had cracked when he said Selene's name—and Grace knew now what her family had erased in silence.

They had called it justice.

But it looked like grief.

And now she had to ask herself a question that made her stomach twist: *Was she here to carry on the legacy... or to end it?*

Her thoughts were interrupted by a faint sound outside—a low growl that sent a shiver down her spine. She turned to Lucas, her hand instinctively brushing against the enchanted bracelet on her wrist.

"Did you hear that?" she whispered.

Lucas's posture shifted instantly, his body tense and alert. His nostrils flared as he sniffed the air, his expression darkening. "We're not alone."

The growl came again, louder this time, followed by the sound of snapping branches. Grace's heart pounded as she drew her silver dagger, her grip tightening around the hilt.

"Stay close," Lucas said, stepping toward the doorway. His movements were fluid and cautious, his eyes scanning the shadows beyond the den.

Before either of them could react, a hulking figure burst through the underbrush, its glowing red eyes locking onto them. The creature was massive, its twisted form a grotesque mockery of a werewolf. Its fur was patchy and matted, and its movements were erratic, as if it were being controlled by something beyond its own will.

"A corrupted one," Lucas growled, his voice low and dangerous.

The creature lunged, its claws raking through the air. Grace barely had time to duck as it crashed into the doorway, splintering wood and sending shards flying.

Lucas moved with lightning speed, grabbing a nearby length of reinforced metal—a relic of the den's former occupants—and swinging it with precision. The blow struck the creature's side, but it barely flinched.

"Selene!" Lucas called, voice cracking through the clearing like a whip.

For a heartbeat, something flickered across the creature's brutalized face—recognition, maybe, or memory—but then the moment snapped. Her great head swung toward Grace, red-ringed eyes blazing with a fury that didn't belong to the sister he remembered.

"Selene, you can fight it," Lucas pleaded, voice breaking. "Come back to us. She's a friend."

But Selene showed no sign of hearing him beyond the first desperate call of her name.

She was terrible and beautiful all at once—sculpted muscle rippling under black fur threaded with streaks of silver and tan, every line of her a hymn to violence. Her eyes, fever-bright and ringed in blood, locked onto Grace. Lips peeled back to reveal teeth as long as Grace's hand, slick and sharp.

Selene crouched low, muscles coiled tight, ready to spring—a predator poised for the killing strike.

Grace heard Virgil's voice in her head, cold and clinical: *Wolves go for the soft parts—the throat, the belly. They bleed you before they break you.*

Selene didn't look like she wanted to bleed her prey.

She looked ready to tear and tear and tear until nothing was left.

She looked like death made flesh. Wild. Free. Irrevocable.

"Go for the legs!" Lucas shouted, his voice ragged with something deeper than fear—resignation.

In that moment, Grace saw it too: the shattering of hope in his eyes, the acceptance that—for now—his sister was lost.

Grace didn't hesitate.

She darted to the side, her silver dagger catching the moonlight in a quick flash. The movement triggered the beast's instincts—its muscles coiled and bunched, the attack written in every taut line of its body.

Selene lunged.

Grace waited—heart pounding, every nerve screaming—until the last possible moment, then dropped into a hard roll beneath the snapping jaws. She slashed upward as she passed, her blade biting deep into the flesh behind Selene's front leg.

A snarl split the night, sharp and furious, but Grace was already moving—already scrambling to her feet, breath ragged, the copper tang of adrenaline flooding her mouth.

Selene howled in pain, its movements faltering. Lucas seized the opportunity, driving the metal bar into its shoulder with a grunt of effort. The impact forced the beast back, but it only seemed to enrage it further. It lashed out wildly, its claws catching Lucas's side and sending him sprawling.

"Lucas!" Grace yelled, rushing to his side. Blood stained his shirt, but he pushed himself up, his expression grim.

"I'm fine," he said through gritted teeth. "Focus on the fight."

Selene charged again, its movements uncoordinated but no less deadly. Grace and Lucas worked together in a chaotic dance of strikes and dodges, each trying to outmaneuver her. The wards on the walls pulsed faintly, reacting to the creature's presence, but their power was weak—fading remnants of what had once been a powerful shield.

Finally, Grace saw her opening.

Selene reared back, muscles bunching for another strike—and Grace lunged forward with everything she had, driving her dagger deep into the creature's chest.

The silver hissed as it met corrupted flesh, a terrible, searing sound. Selene let out a raw, gurgling snarl, her massive body convulsing violently against the blow.

Lucas moved without hesitation, grabbing a metal bar from the wreckage nearby and slamming it down across Selene's shoulders, forcing her to the ground.

Together, straining against her thrashing limbs, they pinned her. Grace could feel the tremor of Selene's rage, the wild, frantic pulse of her heartbeat—but it was weakening.

The corruption seemed to bleed from her with every second the silver stayed buried.

With a final shuddering breath, Selene went still.

Not dead. Not remotely.

The wound would close. The corruption would heal her. The creature beneath their hands still breathed—and would rise again unless given a death she might not come back from.

Grace tightened her grip on the dagger hilt. Lucas leaned heavier into the bar.

Neither of them moved to take the killing blow.

Not yet.

The silence after the struggle was deafening.

Grace collapsed onto her knees, chest heaving, the silver dagger slipping from her blood-slicked fingers. Her whole body trembled, lungs dragging in air that tasted of copper and ash.

Across the room, Lucas sagged against the wall, his face pale, his lips bloodless. His green eyes burned like emerald stars beneath the messy fall of his dark hair—brilliant and broken all at once.

"How do we..." Grace rasped, forcing the words past the rawness in her throat. "How do we contain her?"

Lucas dragged a shaking hand through his curls, already calculating even through the horror.

"If I tie the pipe in—" he started, but a low whine cut him off.

They turned.

And saw what remained.

Where the monstrous wolf had lain, there was now a slight woman pinned to the ground by the twisted iron and the searing bite of silver—bloodied, battered, barely breathing. Skin torn. Limbs trembling.

Selene.

Her human form was fragile and brutalized, but there was no mistaking her.

She lifted her head with a trembling effort, dark hair clinging to her cheeks, and opened her eyes—

Eyes as green as Lucas's.

But threaded through with a fevered, traitorous red.

And when she spoke, her voice was little more than a broken gasp.

"Lucas."

But streaked through with a fevered, unnatural red.

Her mouth moved around his name.

"Lucas," she breathed, voice ragged, a child's whimper in a woman's ruined body.

Something inside Grace broke.

She stepped back.

Not in fear—but in respect.

In horror.

In grief.

This wasn't her moment.

This was theirs.

Lucas dropped to his knees beside his sister, his hands hovering uselessly in the air—afraid to touch, afraid to let go. His lips parted, but whatever words he tried to find tangled and died on his tongue.

Selene reached for him—weak, twitching fingers brushing his wrist.

He caught her hand, swallowed a broken sound, and pressed his forehead to hers.

For a moment, they stayed like that.

Two broken creatures, clinging to the memory of something already lost.

Grace turned away.

She didn't see Lucas make the choice.

She only heard the soft, wet gasp—the stifled, final breath—and the sound of iron dragging across stone.

She didn't know how long she waited, arms wrapped around herself, trying to hold something inside her from shattering completely.

When Lucas came to her, he wasn't whole anymore.

His clothes were stained. His hands trembled. His eyes were wide and hollow, rimmed red with more than blood.

He stopped a few feet away, looking at her like he didn't know how to begin.

"She called my name," he said, voice cracked and raw. "She remembered me."

Grace crossed the space between them without thinking, reaching for his hands, grounding him.

"I'm so sorry," she whispered.

Lucas leaned into her touch like he might break if she let go.

"She remembered," he said again, softer this time.

And Grace held him as the night swallowed the rest.

"They're getting worse," he said finally, his voice filled with quiet anger. "The corruption is spreading faster than I thought."

Grace stared at the creature's lifeless form, her mind racing. This wasn't just a fight for survival—it was something far darker, something her family's teachings had never prepared her for.

"We need to stop this," she said, her voice trembling but resolute. "Before it's too late."

Lucas met her gaze, his green eyes filled with a mixture of gratitude and determination. "Then we'll fight together."

As the moonlight bathed the abandoned den, Grace felt the weight of her choice settle over her. She had crossed a line tonight, and there was no going back.

CHAPTER 9

Grace sat cross-legged on the floor of the den, her silver dagger resting at her side. The dim light of the moon filtered through the cracks in the walls, casting soft beams over Lucas as he leaned against the far wall, his shirt torn and bloodied. His sharp features were drawn tight with pain, but he said nothing, focusing instead on the faintly glowing wards etched into the den's structure.

"You're bleeding," Grace said, breaking the silence. Her voice was steadier than she felt, though her gaze lingered on the gash across his ribs. "Let me see."

"I'm fine," Lucas muttered, brushing off her concern.

"You're not fine." Grace rose and crossed the space between them, kneeling beside him. "If that gets infected, you won't be much use to anyone."

Lucas raised an eyebrow, a faint smirk tugging at the corner of his mouth despite his discomfort. "You're bossy, you know that?"

"Call it survival instinct." Grace retrieved a small cloth from her bag, dampening it with water from a flask. "Sit still."

Reluctantly, Lucas lifted his arm, exposing the deep gash along his ribs. Grace winced at the sight of the torn flesh but said nothing as she worked, cleaning the wound with gentle but firm movements.

"You've done this before," he observed, his voice softer now.

"My family trains us for everything," she replied. "Even basic field medicine. You never know when a hunt will go wrong."

"Seems like they trained you well," Lucas said, his tone thoughtful. "But something tells me you don't always follow the rules."

Grace paused, her hand hovering over his wound. "What's that supposed to mean?"

Lucas met her gaze, his green eyes piercing. "You hesitated tonight. You could've killed that thing outright, but you didn't. Why?"

Grace's stomach tightened. She didn't want to admit it, but she had hesitated. Something about the corrupted werewolf's twisted, pained movements had made her falter—made her wonder if there was still something salvageable beneath the corruption.

"It didn't feel right," she said finally, her voice barely above a whisper. "I've seen werewolves before, but this was... different. It wasn't just a monster. It was suffering."

Lucas nodded slowly, as though he understood. "You're right. The corruption twists everything. It takes what we are and makes it worse. Harsher. More violent."

He shifted slightly, wincing as the movement pulled at his wound. Grace resumed her work, dabbing at the blood and wrapping the injury with a strip of fabric from her bag.

"What happened to Selene?" she asked, her voice careful. "You said she was fighting it. How did it start?"

Lucas let out a heavy sigh, his gaze drifting to the glowing wards on the wall. "Selene was always the strongest of us. Smarter, faster... more controlled. But the curse, it—" He stopped, his jaw tightening as if the words were too painful to say.

"Go on," Grace urged gently.

He exhaled, his voice raw with emotion. "The curse changes us, even without the corruption. The full moon, the transformation—it takes a toll on the mind. But Selene was different. She kept control longer than most of us. Until she didn't."

His hands curled into fists, his knuckles turning white. "She started losing herself. First it was little things—mood swings, lapses in memory. Then came the anger, the violence. She fought it for as long as she could, but the corruption... it's like it was waiting for her to slip. And when it did, it took everything."

Grace's chest ached at the pain in his voice. "Where is she now?"

Lucas shook his head. "I don't know. She's out there somewhere, lost in the woods or hiding in the shadows. I've been tracking her, trying to reach her, but every time I get close..." He trailed off, his expression darkening. "She's not my sister anymore. Not really. She's something else."

For a moment, the only sound in the den was the distant rustle of leaves outside. Grace finished tying the bandage around Lucas's ribs, her hands lingering for a moment before she sat back.

"I can't promise anything," she said carefully, her voice steady. "But I'll think about it. About helping you."

Lucas looked at her, something like relief flickering in his eyes. "That's all I can ask."

The weight of their shared silence was heavy but not uncomfortable. Grace leaned back against the wall, her thoughts a whirlwind of doubt and determination. She had been taught her entire life that werewolves were monsters to be hunted, not people to be saved. But

Lucas's pain, his desperation, had shaken that belief to its core.

If she helped him, she would be defying everything her family stood for. But if she didn't...

The image of the corrupted werewolf flashed in her mind, its twisted form a stark reminder of what could happen if she turned away.

"Get some rest," she said finally, breaking the silence. "You'll need your strength if we're going to figure this out."

Lucas gave her a faint smile, his weariness evident. "You're bossy *and* persistent."

"Goodnight, Lucas," Grace said, unable to hide the hint of a smile.

As the moonlight filtered through the cracks in the den's walls, Grace knew one thing for certain: her life was no longer her own. Whatever came next, she was bound to it—and to him.

The forest was quiet, save for the soft crunch of Grace's boots against the mossy ground. The cool night air wrapped around her like a cloak, carrying with it the earthy scent of damp leaves and pine. The moon hung high above, its silver light filtering through the branches and casting soft shadows along her path.

Her thoughts churned as she walked, a whirlwind of conflicting emotions she couldn't seem to escape. The fight with the corrupted werewolf was still fresh in her mind—the raw chaos, the desperate teamwork, the way Lucas had fought with a precision and resolve that was almost human. Almost.

And then there was the way he had spoken about his sister, his voice heavy with guilt and longing. Grace couldn't ignore the weight of his words, the pain etched into every line of his face as he described Selene's struggle. It had been a glimpse into something deeper, something that made her chest tighten in ways she didn't fully understand.

She shook her head, trying to clear the thoughts that clung to her like cobwebs. *He's a werewolf,* she reminded herself. *A creature my family has been hunting for generations.*

But that truth no longer felt as solid as it once had. Lucas wasn't what she had been taught to expect. He wasn't mindless, and wasn't driven by instinct alone. He was... complicated. And it was that complexity that left her feeling unsteady, as though the ground beneath her feet had shifted without warning.

Grace stopped at the edge of a small clearing, tilting her head back to look at the sky. The moonlight bathed her face, cool and gentle, and for a moment, the weight in her chest lifted. She closed her eyes, letting the forest's stillness seep into her, though her mind refused to quiet.

She couldn't stop replaying the way Lucas had looked at her, his green eyes filled with an intensity that had left her breathless. He had called her different, and said she saw things her family couldn't. The words had struck a chord she didn't want to acknowledge, yet they lingered all the same.

What am I doing? she thought, her fists clenching at her sides. She had agreed to think about helping him, but what did that even mean? Helping a werewolf—helping Lucas—felt like a betrayal of everything she had been taught. But not helping him...

The memory of the corrupted werewolf surged forward, its twisted form and guttural snarls sending a shiver down her spine. If Lucas was right, if the corruption spread unchecked, it wouldn't just be werewolves who suffered. It would be everyone.

Grace opened her eyes and sighed, the silver light of the moon painting the clearing in soft hues. The forest felt alive around her, it's quiet rhythms a stark contrast to the storm inside her.

Why does he make me feel like this? she wondered, her hand brushing against the bracelet on her wrist. The faint warmth from earlier had faded, leaving only the cool metal against her skin. Lucas's presence had stirred something in her, something she couldn't name—a pull that felt both dangerous and undeniable.

Her thoughts drifted back to his words: *You don't just see monsters.*

Grace shook her head, her lips pressing into a thin line. "I don't even know who I am anymore," she whispered to the empty woods.

She adjusted her bag and resumed walking, her steps slower now, as if the weight of her thoughts was dragging her down. The forest began to thin, and the lights of the Lutteux estate flickered faintly in the distance. The sight of home filled her with both relief and dread.

Her family would never understand what she had done tonight. And if they found out...

Grace exhaled sharply, shoving the thought away. She would deal with that later. For now, she just needed to get through the night.

CHAPTER 10

As she stepped out of the woods and onto the edge of the estate grounds, Grace cast one last glance over her shoulder, her eyes scanning the darkened trees. Lucas was still out there, somewhere, carrying the weight of a burden she was beginning to understand all too well.

And for the first time, she wondered if they weren't so different after all.

The thought lingered—heavy and strange—until a flicker of movement caught her eye.

A single window in the west wing was lit.

Faint, flickering candlelight, not the cold, clean glow of electricity. Grace stilled, her breath fogging in the night air. The rest of the house slept in darkness. That wing had been locked for decades. Until Elyria arrived.

She squinted, watching as a shadow moved past the narrow pane. Slow. Deliberate. A shape cloaked in crimson.

Her aunt.

Grace's stomach turned, unease knotting low in her chest.

What was Elyria doing awake, long past midnight, pacing behind curtains and candlelight like something old and restless?

The forest behind her felt safer by comparison.

Without thinking, Grace took one step toward the house—and stopped. Her fingers brushed the red thread on her wrist, as if it might anchor her to stillness.

Tomorrow, she told herself. *Tonight, she can have her secrets.*

But her feet lingered on the path a little too long.

And behind her, the woods whispered like they were listening.

The Lutteux estate was quiet when Grace stepped through the heavy oak door, but the weight of the house's presence was anything but comforting. The dimly lit foyer, with its ancient wooden beams and walls adorned with family relics, seemed to watch her every move. She shut the door softly behind her, hoping to slip upstairs unnoticed.

"Grace."

Her father's voice cut through the silence like a blade.

She froze, her heart pounding. Turning slowly, she saw him standing in the doorway of the study, his broad shoulders silhouetted by the warm glow of the firelight behind him. His arms were crossed, and his expression was unreadable, but the tension in his stance was unmistakable.

"Come here," he said, his tone leaving no room for argument.

Grace swallowed hard and obeyed, stepping into the study with hesitant steps. The room was lined with shelves of old books and hunting trophies, a testament to the generations of Lutteux hunters who had come before. Her father gestured for her to sit in the worn leather chair opposite his desk.

She perched on the edge of the seat, her fingers gripping the hem of her jacket. "What's going on?" she asked, keeping her voice as neutral as possible.

John Lutteux studied her for a moment, his piercing eyes narrowing slightly. "That's what I'd like to know. You've been distracted lately. Skipping dinner, sneaking out. And tonight, you come home looking like you've been running through the woods. Care to explain?"

Grace's pulse quickened, but she kept her face calm. "I went for a walk," she said, her tone casual. "I needed some air."

"In the Moonlit Forest? Four hours?" he pressed, his voice heavy with suspicion. "You know better than to go out there alone, Grace. It's dangerous. You've been gone for hours. No one knew where you were."

"I can handle myself," she said quickly, regretting the sharpness in her tone the moment the words left her mouth.

"Yes Virgil said you have a newfound passion. You'll need that."

Her father's eyes narrowed further, and he leaned forward, resting his elbows on the desk. "But this isn't about handling yourself. It's about responsibility. You're a Lutteux. Everything you do reflects on this family.

Sneaking off into the woods at night doesn't exactly inspire confidence in your judgment."

The words stung more than she wanted to admit. "I wasn't sneaking off," she said defensively. "I just needed some time to think."

"About what?" he asked, his voice quiet but firm.

Grace hesitated, her mind racing for an answer that wouldn't raise more questions. "About the hunt," she lied. "About everything. You're always saying how important it is to be prepared, and I just... I wanted to make sure I'm ready."

Her father leaned back, his expression softening slightly, though the tension in his shoulders remained. "And are you?"

Grace blinked, caught off guard by the question. "What?"

"Are you ready?" he repeated, his gaze unwavering. "Because from where I'm sitting, it looks like you're distracted. And in our line of work, distractions can get you killed."

The weight of his words settled over her, but she refused to let it show. "I'm ready," she said firmly, meeting his gaze.

For a moment, he said nothing, his eyes searching hers as if trying to uncover the truth. Finally, he nodded, though his expression remained guarded.

"Good," he said, standing. "Because we can't afford mistakes, Grace. Not now. You know of the body?"

"Emily mentioned something…"

"So the gossips already have it ..." A bitter sigh escapes his lips.

For a moment he lost that perfect erect posture behind the massive ironwood desk that had anchored the family study for generations and just looked tired.

Around him, the room whispered of old wars—silver blades mounted on velvet, faded portraits of grim-eyed ancestors, the cracked scrying bowl of Isolde resting in a place of reverence. The air smelled of leather and steel.

"He was a fool," Thomas said, flipping through a weathered journal, his tone flat as frost. "Garran Whitlock. Land speculator. Loudmouth. Thought he could dig up the Hollow's edge for a new development—just west of the refuge line. I told him it was sacred ground. Told him wolves wouldn't tolerate steel roots in their soil."

He finally looked up, and the firelight caught the scar that split his jaw—an old mark of some hunt Grace had never been told the story of.

"They found him yesterday," he went on, voice still low but razor-sharp. "No hands. No tongue. Decapitated. No signs of struggle. Just... gone. Like a message left in pieces."

He closed the journal with a soft *thud*, then laced his fingers together on the desk.

"Some prices are paid in permits," he said. "Others, in blood."

And that was it. No grief. No pity. Just the unspoken warning curling in the silence between them.

"Whatever's on your mind, you need to set it aside and focus on what matters. They have acted and so now must we"

"They?" she asked quietly, already dreading the answer.

"I only know of one plague of monsters around here, don't you?"

Grace nodded, rising from her seat. "I understand." *But what if it were not so simple?*

"Dad? What if it wasn't them?"

"It's always them Grace. They might look like people. Remember they are not."

He didn't move as she turned to leave, his voice stopping her just as she reached the door. "Grace."

She glanced back, her hand resting on the doorframe.

"Your mother and I believe in you," he said, his voice softer now. "But belief only goes so far. Prove you're ready. Show me you're ready."

She nodded again, her chest tight with the weight of his words. "I will," she said, her voice barely above a whisper.

As she climbed the stairs to her room, the tension in her chest refused to ease. Her father's suspicion was palpable, and she knew it wouldn't take much to tip him off. If he found out about her alliance with Lucas—about her doubts, her hesitation—it would shatter everything.

She shut her bedroom door behind her and leaned against it, exhaling shakily. The walls seemed to close in around her, the weight of her family's expectations pressing down like a physical force.

Something moved.

She stiffened—and then spotted it.

Her aunt's pug sat neatly in the middle of the rug, its body perfectly still, its glossy eyes reflecting the flicker of candlelight. It looked almost carved from stone, its tongue lolling in a mockery of a smile.

Grace straightened, every inch of her buzzing with anger she couldn't afford to turn on the people she *should*.

Instead, she turned it on the thing sitting in her room like it belonged there.

"No," she said, voice low and shaking. "Not tonight."

The pug tilted its head, as if amused.

She stepped forward, throwing the door wide.

"Out."

The creature didn't move.

Grace gritted her teeth, every instinct screaming at her that this was more than stubbornness—it was *defiance*.

"I hate you," she hissed under her breath. "I don't know what you are, but I hate you."

The pug's tail flicked once, lazily.

And then, almost lazily, it rose and padded from the room, brushing against her ankles as it passed. Its touch was cold. Knowing.

She slammed the door behind it, harder than necessary.

For a moment, she stood there, breathing hard, heart hammering against her ribs.

But there were bigger problems than familiars and strays.

Her father. Her mother. Virgil.

The family she might already be losing.

Grace shoved the encounter aside, burying it under the avalanche of more immediate fears as she crossed the room and slumped into the chair by the fire.

For the first time, she truly understood the danger of the path she had chosen. She wasn't just walking a fine line—she was balancing on the edge of a blade.

And one wrong step would cut her to the core.

CHAPTER 11

That night, Grace slept without dreams—but not without unease. Her body lay still, cocooned in tangled sheets, but her mind never quite settled. It was like floating just beneath the surface of sleep, where breath comes easy but the air feels too thin. No visions. No voices. Just a weight pressing down on her chest, like the forest was watching her even here. She woke more tired than when she lay down, the absence of dreams somehow more disturbing than their presence.

The Lutteux mansion was unnervingly quiet as Grace made her way down the long hallway to Elyria's quarters. The dimly lit corridor felt colder here, the flickering light from the wall sconces casting elongated shadows that seemed to follow her every step. Elyria lived in the oldest wing of the mansion, a section that the rest of the family avoided, steeped in an air of mystery and latent power.

Grace hesitated at the heavy oak door before knocking lightly. It creaked open almost immediately, as if Elyria had been waiting for her.

"Grace," Elyria greeted, her sharp blue eyes scanning her niece with mild amusement. She stood draped in a deep green robe, the intricate embroidery shimmering faintly, hinting at spells woven into the fabric. "What brings you here? Trouble with John, I presume?"

In the far corner of the room, the pug was rolling onto its back, stubby legs flailing in the air as it tried—unsuccessfully—to scratch at its own ear. It made a delighted snorting sound, tail wagging in frantic little circles as it squirmed like any ordinary, spoiled lapdog. But when it stopped, mid-wiggle, its head lolled unnaturally to the side—and its eyes locked onto Grace without blinking. The tail kept wagging. The grin stayed fixed. But the stillness behind that look made the back of her neck prickle.

Grace stepped inside, the warmth of the room wrapping around her. The scent of herbs and old books mingled with the faint crackle of the fire in the hearth. Elyria's quarters were a blend of the arcane and the domestic, shelves brimming with jars of strange ingredients, ancient tomes, and trinkets that seemed to hum with latent magic.

"Something like that," Grace admitted, sitting at the worn, intricately carved table near the fire. "I need answers. About our family. About the curse."

Elyria's expression turned serious, the humor evaporating from her features. She closed the door behind her and gestured for Grace to continue. "The curse is a heavy burden, Grace. One your father prefers to see as black and white. Why come to me?"

Grace hesitated, her fingers twisting the hem of her sleeve. "I've seen things that don't match what I've been taught. I think there's more to the story than what we've been told."

Elyria tilted her head, studying Grace intently. "And what do you think you've been missing?"

"Everything," Grace said, her voice trembling slightly. "I don't think the curse is what we think it is. And I think you know the truth."

Elyria's lips pressed into a thin line, and she stood abruptly. "Wait here."

Grace watched as her aunt crossed the room to a tall cabinet, its surface carved with symbols that glowed faintly under her touch. She opened it and retrieved a small, leather-bound journal. Its cover was embossed with the initials "I.L." in faded gold lettering.

Elyria set the journal on the table before Grace, her movements deliberate. "If you want the truth, then read. But be warned—what you find will change everything."

Grace's hands trembled as she picked up the journal. The first few entries were mundane, recounting Isolde Lutteux's daily life in the French countryside. But as she turned the pages, her breath quickened.

June 12, 1764

Power. It is the one constant in this world, the force that drives men to war and families to ruin. The Revolution threatens to strip it from us, to leave the Lutteux name as nothing more than whispers in the dark. But I will not allow it. I have discovered a way to ensure our place—magic that will not only preserve our legacy but elevate it.

Grace's stomach twisted as she continued reading. The tone grew darker, the handwriting more frantic.

August 1, 1764

The ritual was a success. The creatures are more than I could have imagined—beasts born of shadow and fury, bound by my will. They will secure our family's dominion, protect us from those who would tear us down. But the cost... I underestimated it.

Her chest tightened. The creatures Isolde described—there was no mistaking what they were. Werewolves.

She created them.

Grace turned the pages faster now, her eyes scanning the hurried, ink-stained words.

October 5, 1764

It is unraveling. The creatures are uncontrollable, their power far greater than I anticipated. They obey no master, not even me. They are no longer protectors—they are predators. I have created monsters, and they will destroy us all unless I stop them.

We must flee. I have bound our bloodline to a solemn pledge: to undo what I have done, to destroy the creatures born of my hubris. The Lutteux name will no longer command power but atone for it. We are hunters now, protectors of the balance I shattered.

Grace's hands fell to her lap, the journal slipping from her fingers onto the table. She looked up at Elyria, her voice barely a whisper. "She made them."

Elyria nodded, her expression calm but solemn. "Yes. Isolde's ambition was her undoing. She created the curse to elevate our family, to make us untouchable. But the creatures she birthed were too powerful, too wild to control. So she bound us to them—to destroy what she had created."

Grace's mind raced. Her family's legacy wasn't one of nobility or honor. It was one of penance and desperation, an endless cycle of atonement for a sin none of them had committed.

Grace stumbled back, the world tilting. The study spun around her in slow, nauseating circles—portraits of long-dead Lutteux matriarchs watching from the walls with eyes too knowing, too cold. The fire snapped in the hearth, but the warmth didn't reach her. Not now.

She pressed her hands to her temples as if she could hold the truth out—*as if denial could drown lineage.* But it didn't stop. It poured through her like floodwater. The wolf kneeling in her dream. The way corrupted wolves hesitated near her. The way Lucas had looked at her—not with fear, but recognition.

Isolde. The blood-witch. The architect of the curse. The reason entire generations howled at the moon until their minds tore themselves apart.

Her ancestor.

Grace couldn't breathe. Her chest rose in short, panicked gasps, and her silver bracelet burned against her wrist like it was branding her, not blessing her.

She had thought the Lutteux were hunters. Protectors.

But they were the architects of damnation. And she—the girl who'd tried so hard to be brave, to be *good*—was just another link in a cursed chain.

"No," she whispered. "No, no, no."

Her legs moved before she could think, boots striking the hallway stone like thunder. Past the portraits. Past the ancestral blades. Past her mother's cry of alarm.

She ran from the house and into the forest, the early dawn swallowing her whole, because staying would mean accepting the truth.

And the truth was *monstrous*.

The trees tore at her like hands.

Branches clawed at Grace's sleeves as she stumbled deeper into the woods, the moon veiled behind a smear of clouds. Her breath came in ragged sobs, fogging in the cold night air, each step more desperate than the last. The forest floor blurred beneath her—mud, roots, broken leaves—and still she ran. The early morning darkness felt alive, like it *knew* her name now, like it had been waiting for her.

She didn't care where she was going. She just had to outrun it—the blood in her veins, the legacy in her name, the horror twisting through her ribcage like wire. *Isolde's curse. Her curse.* It wasn't just in the wolves. It was in her. And it had always been.

Footsteps behind her. Fast. Steady.

She whipped around mid-stride, heart leaping into her throat, hand flying to her dagger—but it wasn't a threat. It was *him*. Lucas. Half-shadow, half-boy, eyes glowing faintly in the gloom.

He didn't say her name. He didn't have to.

"I said stay away," she gasped, not even knowing if she'd said it aloud before.

But Lucas kept pace beside her, not reaching, not speaking—just *running* with her now, their steps in sync, the silence between them cracked wide with emotion.

She stopped suddenly, nearly collapsing, one hand bracing against a moss-slicked tree trunk. Her breath hitched. She hated him in that moment—for being calm, for understanding, for seeing her when she wanted to disappear.

And then she screamed.

"My family did this!"

The words ripped out of her like a wound. "We made the curse. We *cursed* you. All of you. All this time I thought we were fighting it—and we're the ones who started it. Do you understand how *fucking wrong* that is?"

Lucas stepped forward, slow and quiet, until the space between them thinned to nothing. He didn't flinch when her fists hit his chest. He just stood there, solid as stone, until her anger melted into sobs and she collapsed against him.

The silver bracelet at her wrist burned cold—a reminder of bloodlines and oaths. But pressed against Lucas, it felt like it was pulsing. Not in pain. In resonance.

She didn't expect him to hold her.

But he did.

His arms wrapped around her like they were built for it, steady and trembling all at once. His scent—earth, ash, the faintest trace of something wild—settled into her lungs like truth.

His hand moved to her hair, slow and careful, and his voice when it came was almost reverent.

"You didn't choose this legacy, Grace."

Her breath hitched. "But it chose me."

"And maybe," he said, pulling her just slightly closer, "you're the one who breaks it."

She stayed there, folded into him beneath the watching trees, her body shaking, his heartbeat steady against her cheek.

The forest held its breath.

And somewhere far above them, the clouds shifted, letting the moon bear witness.

The silence between them deepened—not heavy now, but *charged*. Grace's breathing had steadied into uneven tremors, her face still damp, flushed from crying. She became suddenly, painfully aware of how close they were.

Of the way her forehead rested against his chest.
 Of how warm he was—unnaturally so—and how solid he felt beneath her hands.
 Of how her fingers had curled, unconsciously, into the fabric of his shirt.

And worse—how he didn't seem to mind.

His arms hadn't moved away. If anything, they'd drawn her in closer, his thumb now brushing a slow, steady rhythm across her back. Not possessive. Not comforting in the way her family did it. But something else—something slower. *Watching.*

She swallowed hard, pulling back a fraction, just enough to tilt her head. Her eyes met his.

The forest didn't matter. The curse didn't matter. For one moment, all she could feel was the burn of her flushed cheeks and the maddening thrum in her wrist where her bracelet rested between them—pressed to his skin.

Lucas's expression didn't shift. But his eyes did.

Softer now. Curious. A little wild around the edges. And entirely unreadable.

Grace suddenly didn't know if she was trembling from the crying... or from *this*.

CHAPTER 12

In the end, Grace had run away from him too.

From the boy who smelled of pine and wolf, whose eyes saw through every wall she thought she'd built. She'd left him in the dark, beneath trees that listened, heart pounding with something she hadn't dared to name.

Morning hit her like a cold slap.

She moved on instinct—brushed her hair, pulled on clothes, blinked past the weight of her dreamless night. But as she stepped outside, the sun was already too high, she remembered.

The note.

Her stomach dropped. Her feet moved.

She ran—not because of monsters this time, but because of the girl who *would have read it.*

Emily.

She was already waiting by Grace's locker, arms crossed tight, eyes wide with a fury that only came from *fear.*

"You did, didn't you," Emily said, her voice low and shaking. "You took that step."

Grace opened her mouth. Closed it. Nodded.

Emily stared at her for a long, loaded breath.

Then: "May the Goddess help you."

The words weren't dramatic. They were *true*. Like a prayer, or a curse, or both.

Grace looked at her—really looked—and saw the worry, the heartbreak, the loyalty barely holding itself together.

"I came back," she said quietly.

"For now," Emily replied, not unkindly. "But how many steps until you don't?"

Emily skipped class. Jenna was gone. With no friend and no enemy, Grace drifted through the day like smoke—formless, untethered. She floated from one class to the next, barely hearing the lessons, her body present but her mind ghosted. No one spoke to her. The students shifted around her in the halls like water parting around a stone. They didn't know why they avoided her, not consciously—but they *felt* it. Something in her had changed. And whatever it was, it unnerved them. She was marked now—by blood, by silence, by something they couldn't name. And they wanted none of it.

The school gates squealed shut behind her, but Grace didn't flinch.

The day had left her hollow—no Emily, no Jenna, no one willing to meet her gaze. Her footsteps echoed on the pavement, her bag hanging loose off one shoulder, the red thread at her wrist frayed and damp with sweat.

She almost didn't see him.

Virgil stepped out from where he waited, arms folded across his chest, leaning against their father's car like he'd been carved from the stone steps of the manor itself.

"Get in," he said, without greeting.

She stopped short. "What are you doing here?"

He didn't move. "Emily came to me."

Grace's heart sank.

"She said you left a note. Said you've been acting strange. Said you came back from something—but you weren't the same."

He opened the passenger door with a click that felt too loud in the fading light.

"I'm listening now, Grace. Talk."

So she did.

She told him about Lucas. About the meeting at the woods' edge, the blood-deep pull that had nothing to do with fear. About what she'd seen in his eyes—*not corruption. Not monstrosity. Humanity.* She spoke of her doubt in the family legacy, her horror at the executioner's blade that had been passed down like an heirloom. Her voice shook. But she didn't stop.

When she finished, she waited.

Virgil didn't speak.

Not at first.

Then: "You met with *a cursed wolf* and *hid it from us*?"

His voice was soft. Too soft.

"Virgil—"

"You walked into the woods. Alone. With *him*." His hands curled into fists. "And now you come back spinning stories about broken legacies and *feelings*?"

"I'm trying to understand—"

"No," he snapped. "You're trying to rewrite your blood."

Before she could protest, he grabbed her arm—not roughly, not yet—and pulled her toward the car.

"Stop it!" she yelled, trying to wrench away. "You said you'd listen!"

"I did." His eyes were cold, his voice iron. "And now I'm acting."

The ride home was silent.

Grace sat stiff in her seat, breathing hard, too angry to cry, too afraid to speak.

When they reached the house, he didn't take her to Marielle. He didn't shout. He walked her to her room, pushed her inside, and shut the door behind her.

The *click* of the lock was soft.

But it rang louder than any scream.

Marielle came to Grace's room. She didn't knock.

She found Grace sitting on the floor by the window, the journal open beside her, her boots still on.

"I'm not here to argue," Marielle said, gently closing the door behind her.

Grace stepped inside, not bothering to hide her fury. "You tell me. What else are we hiding?"

Marielle closed the book with deliberate care. "You'll need to be more specific."

Grace dropped her bag onto the side table and pulled the journal free, holding it out like an accusation. "Isolde's journal. I know what she did. She didn't just fight the cursed—she *made* them. This legacy? It's not justice. It's a cover-up."

Marielle's face didn't flinch, but her eyes darkened, and her mouth flattened into a thin, brittle line. "Where did you find that?"

"Does it matter?" Grace snapped. "Why didn't you tell me?"

Marielle rose slowly, the firelight painting her face in amber and shadow. "Because some truths bury deeper than bones. Because knowing it won't unmake what's already been set in motion."

Grace's voice broke. "But it could've changed *everything.*"

Marielle crossed to her, her voice quiet, even as her presence filled the room. "Changed what, Grace? The wolves are still cursed. The blood still calls. You still carry a dagger on your hip."

Grace shook her head, jaw tight. "You knew and you said nothing. You let us believe we were righteous."

"We are *necessary*," Marielle said, and there was steel in it. "The curse didn't end with Isolde. It didn't vanish with her guilt. It grew. It *learned*. It watches us, waits for weakness. If we lay down our blades, it will devour everything we've tried to hold back."

"And if we keep them raised?" Grace countered. "How much blood is enough, Mom? How many wolves do we kill before we admit we're just fueling it?"

Marielle's gaze softened, grief curling at the corners of her mouth. "Isolde tried to end it, Grace. She failed. And nearly took the family with her."

"So we keep failing, just more quietly?" Grace's voice trembled. "I won't."

Silence swelled between them like smoke.

Then Marielle said, "You've always had a strong heart. But strong hearts bruise easier."

"I'd rather bruise than blindfold myself."

Grace turned and walked out, the journal heavy in her hand, her mother's voice chasing her softly down the corridor:

"Be careful, Grace. The curse is always watching."

"Your father is stern, he has to be with this weight but he's worried about you."

Grace's laugh was hollow. "Dad's never worried about anything but family honor."

"You are wrong, you are his family," Marielle said, quietly. "So is Virgil. They care, they boss. That doesn't make them right. But they boss because they care."

Grace looked up then, eyes sharp with something close to defiance. "Then they should hear the truth."

Marielle met her gaze.

"I want to convene the hunters," Grace said. "Call a council. Speak plainly. Tell them what I found. What we are."

Marielle blinked, once. "That's a foolish idea."

"But it's my right," Grace said, rising. "I'm blooded. I took the vow. I bear the mark. Whether you like it or not."

A long pause. Then Marielle nodded, just once. "Yes. You're blooded. It *is* your right."

She stepped forward and placed a hand lightly on Grace's shoulder.

"Just... be ready for what they'll do with your truth."

Grace covered her mother's hand with her own.

"I already am."

Grace sat cross-legged on the floor of her room, the journal spread open in her lap. Most of the pages were brittle and ink-stained, the script growing messier the deeper she went. But near the end, pressed between pages warped with old water damage and something darker, she found the entry.

The words were shaky, the lines crowded, like Isolde had written them in a rush—*or through tears.*

"I loved him.

That is the truth I can no longer silence.

Before the curse. Before the blood and the madness. I loved him with a soul not meant for power, but I tried to save him all the same. That was my first mistake.

Love made me reckless. Grief made me cruel.

I wove the curse to bring him back—to *bind* him to this world. But I underestimated what hatred does when it becomes immortal. The curse did not save him. It *consumed* him. And I chained my blood to its teeth.

To my children... I am sorry.

To those who bear my name... I am sorry.

This legacy of silver and silence was never meant to become doctrine. It was penance. And I failed even at that.

I pray you will be braver than I was. That you will love without trying to cage it. That you will fight without forgetting who you fight *for*.

Break it, if you can.

Be stronger than me."

—

Grace's throat tightened. She read it again.

And again.

The final words were a whisper in faded ink, barely legible now. But she could feel them, branded into the page—and into her bones.

CHAPTER 13

The Lutteux manor had not seen a full assembly of hunters in decades.

They arrived just after dusk, their boots silent on stone, their eyes sharp as blades. Hoods pulled low. Coats smelling of damp leaves, iron, and long-polished silver. They came not as neighbors or kin, but as soldiers summoned by legacy—and suspicion.

Candles lined the hallways, guttering in unseen drafts. The fire in the great hearth was too low to warm the room, casting long shadows that twisted behind every chair. They gathered in a crescent around the hearth—Thomas, Virgil, Alex, Rhea, old Garin from the western reaches, and a dozen others, some of whom Grace barely remembered.

They didn't sit.

Hunters never sat unless they *had* to.

At the front of the room, Grace stood alone.

Not Marielle. Not Thomas. *Her.*

She wore black. Not mourning—*reclamation.* Her red thread bracelet still bound at her wrist, the silver dagger at her side gleaming dully under the firelight. Isolde's journal was pressed to her chest like scripture.

The room waited, full of heat and tension and breath that didn't move.

Grace swallowed once, then raised her voice.

"Thank you for coming."

No one answered.

She continued anyway.

"I called this assembly not as a daughter, or a girl, or a sister—but as a blooded hunter. As is my right."

A few of them shifted at that—surprised, maybe, that she'd invoke the old law so directly.

"I've read Isolde's journal."

Now the room reacted. Sharply. Some stiffened. Others scoffed. Alex actually muttered, *"Blasphemy."*

Grace raised her voice.

"She was not who we were told. She created the curse. Not out of malice—but out of grief. She loved someone and tried to save him, and in doing so, she damned herself. And us."

"You're asking us to pity the mother of monsters?" Garin growled.

"I'm asking you to *listen.*"

Virgil crossed his arms. "To what? That we've been living a lie? That the wolves we've fought and buried and bled for are just victims of a broken-hearted witch?"

"They *are* victims," Grace snapped. "But so are we. The curse feeds on fear. On pain. It wants us locked in this war. Isolde saw it. And she tried to undo it. Her final words—"

She opened the journal, her hands trembling.

"—were *Break it, if you can. Be stronger than me.*"

Silence followed. It was not kind.

Thomas stepped forward. "And what would you have us do, Grace? Let the wolves roam? Wait until the next child is torn apart in their sleep? What is your grand solution?"

Grace opened her mouth—

—and nothing came out.

She didn't have one.

Not yet.

She looked at them—at the people who had raised her, trained her, mourned with her. And killed beside her. People hardened by loss. People who *needed* the violence to mean something.

"I don't know," she admitted softly. "I don't know what comes next. But I know this can't be all there is."

She looked down at the journal, then back up.

"She asked us to be better. Not because it was easy—but because she failed. I'm not standing here asking you to forgive the wolves. I'm asking you to listen before you strike. To *see* before you condemn."

The fire hissed.

Outside, the wind howled through the trees, rattling the windows like bones.

Rhea was the first to speak.

"If you're wrong," she said, "people will die."

"If I'm right," Grace replied, "they won't have to."

More silence.

Then Marielle stepped forward—not beside Grace, but *behind* her.

She didn't speak. She just stood there, hands folded, eyes unreadable.

One by one, the others turned toward Thomas.

He didn't nod.

But he didn't object.

And for now, that was enough.

Grace bowed her head.

Somewhere just beyond the manor walls, the night seemed to hold its breath.

The knock was soft—barely more than a whisper against the door.

Grace didn't answer.

She sat curled on the edge of her bed, the journal open in her lap, the words swimming in candlelight. Her head throbbed with half-formed thoughts, doubts with too many teeth, and a hollow ache beneath her ribs that wouldn't leave.

The door creaked open anyway.

Elyria stepped inside, her crimson robe trailing behind her like spilled ink, eyes shadowed but unreadable. Her pug followed at her heels, snorting and huffing like an ugly shadow, its nails clicking too sharply against the wooden floor.

"I thought you might be awake," she said, her voice low. Gentle. "I felt you wouldn't be sleeping."

Grace didn't speak. Her fingers tightened around the edge of the journal.

Elyria moved closer, slow and careful, like approaching a wounded animal. "You've been carrying so much, little star. The weight of it is starting to bend you."

"I'm fine," Grace muttered, but even she didn't believe it.

Elyria sat beside her on the bed, leaving a breath of space between them. The pug settled near the fire, its eyes on them unnaturally attentive.

"I know what you saw in him," she said softly. "And I know what you fear now. That if the hunters are right, you'll lose him. That if *I'm* right... you might lose yourself."

Grace's throat tightened.

"I don't want to lose anyone else," she whispered.

Elyria nodded, resting her hands in her lap. "Then let me help."

Grace turned to her, wary. "Help how?"

"The ritual I tried before—it was wrong. Rushed. Incomplete." Her voice remained calm, convincing. "But I've refined it. Adjusted the flow. The moon is full tomorrow night, and if we act then, I believe I can cleanse the curse. Not just suppress it. *Cure it.*"

Grace stared at her.

"All of them?" she asked.

Elyria nodded once. "Yes. Lucas. Selene. The whole pack."

The silence that followed was sharp.

"I don't know if I trust you," Grace admitted.

"You don't have to," Elyria said. "You just have to believe there's still something left worth saving."

Grace looked down at her bracelet. The red thread pulsed faintly, as if aware.

"Let me speak to him," she said quietly. "If we do this—it has to be *his* choice."

Elyria smiled, slow and soft. "Of course."

She rose, gliding toward the door. "But don't wait too long. The curse doesn't sleep forever."

The door closed behind her with a quiet click.

Grace sat alone in the candlelight, the journal still open on her lap, the ghosts of Isolde's regrets whispering around her.

And for the first time, she wondered if hope was just another kind of hunger.

Grace lay in her bed, her mind drifting into the hazy territory of dreams. The night was unusually quiet, with only the distant rustling of trees and the occasional murmur of wind through the open window. In her sleep, the shadows shifted, pulling her into a world that was not her own.

In this dreamscape, she found herself in a mist-covered forest, the air thick with the scent of pine and earth. The moon hung low and full, casting silver light across the scene. In the distance, two figures emerged from the shadows: a woman, strong and regal, with flowing dark hair that caught the moonlight, and a figure beside her—tall, powerful, and yet somehow wild. His features were both human and beast, his eyes glinting with an almost primal hunger.

Isolde, the woman, approached him with a grace that belied the storm within her, her fingers brushing lightly against his arm. The werewolf, the first of his kind, looked at her not with the detached gaze of one who keeps their distance, but with something deeper, something intimate. Their eyes locked, and in that fleeting moment, Grace could feel the pull between them—a bond not of fear, but of something far more dangerous, more thrilling.

Their lips met—soft at first, then fierce, like two storms colliding in a desperate, tender chaos. The kiss was both an invitation and a surrender, a dance of power and vulnerability. Grace felt her breath catch in her chest, as though she, too, had been kissed by the storm.

And then, as quickly as it had come, the vision shifted. The scene blurred and twisted, leaving only the lingering taste of that kiss in her mind. The dream began to fade, but not without leaving something behind—a feeling of longing. Of something she could almost touch but was too far away to grasp.

Grace awoke with a start, her heart beating faster than it should have. The room was dark, the only light coming from the faintest sliver of moonlight that crept through the curtains. She drew a shaky breath, trying to ground herself in reality. But there was a feeling—a spark—that she couldn't shake.

She closed her eyes again, half-expecting to see the dream continue. She thought of Lucas, of the way he moved so confidently, the way he held himself, always just a little bit apart, as though there was a secret he carried with him. Grace wondered what it would be like if the storm of that first kiss was not just a memory from a dream. What if it were real?

But no. She shook her head, letting the thought slip away. She wasn't like Isolde. She wasn't meant for a world so untamed, so full of fire. Yet... there was a part of her that wanted to be. Wanted to know what it felt like to give in to something that wild, that free.

A soft sigh escaped her lips, and she let the dream linger in the back of her mind as she drifted back into an uneasy sleep.

CHAPTER 14

The Lutteux training hall was filled with the rhythmic clang of steel as Grace entered. The vast room, lined with racks of weapons and walls adorned with trophies from past hunts, smelled faintly of oil and aged wood. Virgil stood at the far end, his shirt damp with sweat, methodically swinging a weighted practice blade. His movements were sharp and deliberate, each strike landing with a precision that spoke to years of experience.

Grace hesitated, her fingers tightening around the strap of her bag. She hadn't come here to argue, but the weight of Isolde's journal in her pack—and the questions it raised—made her restless. Virgil turned, catching sight of her as she stepped closer.

"Well, if it isn't the prodigal hunter," he drawled, setting the blade down with a clang. "Did you come to watch, or are you planning to actually practice for once? Or do you have more speeches for us?"

A few heads turned.

She hadn't noticed how full the hall was. A knot of younger hunters—some cousins, some apprentices barely sixteen—stood nearby, sparring with dulled blades. Abby was among them, tightening her gloves, her eyes narrowed and unreadable. Rhea leaned against the wall with her arms folded, watching everything with a disapproving stare.

Grace stepped onto the mat.

"I came to train," she said, slipping off her bag and setting it gently by the edge. "And to talk."

One of the younger hunters—Alaric, a cousin from the east branch—smirked as he twirled his staff. "About wolves again?"

Another, Mara, hesitated. "I heard she saw one shift. Said it wasn't... corrupted."

"That true?" someone asked.

Grace looked around, heart pounding, but steady. "It is."

A long silence.

Then Virgil picked up a second blade and tossed it at her feet. "Fine. Let's talk while you bleed."

They circled each other. The others watched, the clatter of training weapons quieting as eyes turned to the center of the hall.

"You're going to get someone killed," Virgil hissed, low enough only she could hear. "You're planting doubt in the next generation before they've even survived a real hunt."

"They deserve the truth," Grace said, parrying his first strike. "Not the version we've been fed."

"You think what we've done isn't truth?"

"I think it's only half of it."

Their blades clashed again, harder this time.

"Isolde made the curse," Grace said, loud enough for others to hear. "She bound it to our bloodline. She regretted it. And we've been killing ever since to pretend that guilt means righteousness."

A few gasps. Abby's hand froze halfway to her belt.

"Lies," Rhea snapped from the wall. "Blasphemy."

But Mara stepped forward. "Then let her finish."

Grace turned toward her, surprised. Mara's expression was uncertain, but her stance was firm.

"She's not asking us to drop our blades," Mara said. "She's asking us to *think* before we use them."

Alaric muttered, "Thinking's what gets people killed."

"No," Grace said, voice rising. "*Not thinking* is what keeps us killing. Over and over. Maybe it's time we ask who benefits from that."

The room went silent again. Virgil stared at her, breathing hard.

Then he looked at the others.

And realized not all of them were looking *at* Grace.

Some were looking *toward* her.

"You think you're too good for the family's duty" he snarled.

"This isn't about me being 'too good,'" Grace snapped. "It's about the truth. Don't you care that everything we've been told is a lie?"

"Of course, I care," Virgil shot back, his voice sharp. "But what difference does it make? We still have a job to do. The werewolves are out there, killing people, spreading their curse. Whether Isolde made them or not doesn't change that."

Grace's hands clenched into fists. "It changes everything. They're not just mindless monsters, Virgil. They didn't ask for this. And maybe, just maybe, we've been so focused on hunting them that we've ignored the bigger picture."

Virgil's eyes narrowed, and he stepped closer, his voice dropping to a low growl. "You think they're victims? You think they deserve compassion? Let me remind you what happens when you hesitate, Grace. Remember that night in the woods? When I had to step in because you froze? Do you remember what it cost me?"

Her chest tightened, guilt surging at his words. The scar that ran across his face, a constant reminder of that night, felt like an accusation she could never escape.

"This isn't about that," she said, her voice trembling. "This is about—"

"This is about survival," Virgil cut her off, his tone ice-cold. "You're too soft, Grace. Always have been. And one day, it's going to get you killed."

Her anger flared, her voice rising. "Maybe I'm soft because I actually think about what we're doing, instead of blindly swinging a sword like you!"

Virgil's expression darkened, but he said nothing, his silence more cutting than any words. The tension between them was thick, the unspoken resentment and bitterness threatening to boil over.

Grace grabbed her bag, slinging it over her shoulder. "You know what? Forget it. Keep telling yourself you're the hero in all this. But someday, you're going to have to face the truth."

She turned on her heel and stormed out, her heart pounding as the door slammed shut behind her. The cool air of the hallway did little to soothe the fire in her chest.

As she made her way toward her room, her mind swirled with frustration and doubt. Virgil's words had struck a nerve, but so had her own. She didn't want to believe he was right—that her compassion was a weakness—but the weight of her family's legacy pressed down on her like a shroud.

For now, all she could do was keep moving forward, even if the path ahead felt more uncertain than ever.

CHAPTER 15

The hike to the refuge blurred past Grace in a fog of nerves and unfinished dreams.

The early morning light filtered through the trees, pale and cold, but her skin burned hotter with every step.

The abandoned camp looked the same — sad and lonely — except for one small, fragile thing:

A fire.

And him.

Lucas sat by the flames, stirring a battered tin mug.

The sharp scent of burnt coffee twisted in the air.

"If you want to creep up on us," he said, voice dry, "you need to be a much quieter little hunter."

He didn't turn.

Didn't need to.

Somehow, he *felt* her there.

The way the fire felt the pull of the night.

"I wasn't creeping," Grace said, trying for irritation, missing it by a mile.

Her voice came out too soft.

Too *breathless*.

"I wanted to talk, wolf-boy."

Lucas tapped the log beside him, a wordless invitation.

Then reached for the kettle again, movements careful.

He seemed... awkward this morning.

Not casual.

Not calm.

Like her.

Grace dropped her bag, the journal inside burning against her spine like a second heartbeat.

The pages inside haunted her — the inked words gnawing through her sleep, the past threading itself into her blood.

It wasn't just history anymore.

It was **hers.**

It was **theirs.**

Beyond the fire, the woods loomed darker than usual.

Colder.

The edges of the world frayed — as if something sacred had already shifted, and she hadn't caught up.

Instinct pulled her closer to the heat.
To the boy — the beast — hunched beside it.

Lucas handed her a tin cup without speaking.
Their fingers brushed — a soft, accidental kiss of skin-on-skin — and **the fire had nothing on the heat that jolted through her.**

Grace sat down stiffly, knees almost brushing his.

His presence was a weight.
A gravity.

She was used to it now, the way the air seemed to warp around him — like he bent the world just by existing.

But today, there was an edge to him.
A tautness that hadn't been there before.

Like the kiss still stretched between them — unseen, unspoken, *undeniable*.

Lucas stilled as she pulled the journal out.

His brow furrowed, the tension spiking sharper.

"Grace?"

His voice, low and rough, brushing over her name like a caress.

"Everything okay?"

She looked up — and for one wild heartbeat, she forgot what she'd meant to say.

The firelight carved his face into sharp gold and shadow.

His eyes — that impossible, soul-breaking green — caught her and *held* her.

Her breath stalled.

Her body remembered the taste of him —

The scrape of his mouth against hers —

The way his hand had cradled her bruised jaw with terrible, trembling care.

Her thighs pressed together reflexively, a desperate, stupid instinct to anchor herself against the ache blooming low in her stomach.

There was so much she didn't understand.

So much she should have feared.

But right now, the only thing she knew — deep in her blood, deep in her bones — was *him*.

"I need to talk to you," she said.

The words shook loose from her like autumn leaves, brittle and trembling.

Lucas shifted — closer without meaning to — his knee bumping hers.

Neither of them moved away.

Grace set the journal aside, her palms flat against her knees like she could hold herself together with sheer force.

The fire snapped, spitting sparks into the cold morning air.

She didn't dare look away from him.

Because if she did —

If she gave herself even an inch —

She would fall straight back into him.

Into the ruin they were already weaving between them.

"I found something," she began, her fingers trembling slightly as she opened the journal again. "Something about Isolde and the curse... and about... me."

Lucas didn't interrupt, though she could see his curiosity flicker in the way he tilted his head. She turned the pages slowly, finding the passage that had unsettled her the most, the one that spoke of the connection between the first werewolf and the woman who had once been his lover—his equal in every sense, until the curse twisted them both.

"Isolde was a part of something bigger," Grace continued, her voice barely above a whisper. "The curse... it's tied to her bloodline, to the first werewolf. They weren't just enemies or allies. They were—" She stopped, swallowing hard. "They were lovers. Isolde and him. And when the curse was born, it took them both.

But it didn't end with them. It's... it's continuing through me."

Lucas shifted slightly, leaning forward, his gaze intense as he listened. "What does that mean, Grace? That it's continuing through you?"

She hesitated, the weight of the words pressing against her chest. "It means I'm part of this curse. It means... Whatever happened to Isolde is somehow tied to me. That whatever she went through, I might be forced to go through, too. And that's not even the worst part. The worst part is that..." She stopped again, her throat tightening. "There's something about the bloodline. Something about the first werewolf. His touch, his bite—it's all connected."

Lucas was quiet for a long moment. Grace could feel the shift in the air, the intensity building between them, until at last, he spoke, his voice low and steady.

"We've always known this was bigger than us," he said, his hand reaching across the table to cover hers. His touch was warm, grounding, but his eyes betrayed his thoughts—thoughts she could only guess at. "This curse—it's not just something we can run from. But we've been walking this path together since the beginning. Whatever happens next... we face it together."

Grace met his gaze, and for a moment, the weight of their shared fate felt more real than ever. The bond between them wasn't just one of circumstance or proximity—it was deeper, older, like something that had always been there, waiting to be discovered.

"Do you think we can break it?" she asked, her voice quiet but desperate for an answer she wasn't sure she even wanted.

Lucas's eyes softened, his thumb brushing lightly over her hand. "I don't know. But I know we'll try. And whatever happens, I'll be right here with you. You're not alone in this."

Grace felt a strange sense of peace in his words, though the uncertainty still gnawed at her. Still, there was something about his presence, something about his unwavering determination, that made the weight of the journal and its revelations a little less heavy.

As their hands remained intertwined, Grace realized that the story of Isolde and the first werewolf was more than just a dark memory of the past—it was a warning. A warning of the power that connected them all, and the choices that lay ahead. And if their destinies were truly intertwined, if they were truly bound by this curse, then there was no escaping it.

But for the first time, Grace allowed herself to hope that maybe, just maybe, the bond they shared could be enough to break the cycle.

"I have something to tell you too," Lucus said, breaking the silence.

"Selene was desperate, you know?" Lucas' voice broke the eerie silence, quiet yet heavy with emotion as he stared into the shadows. "She thought Elyria could help—could save us. But it only made things worse."

Grace, leaning against a moss-covered stone, wrapped her arms around herself as if to ward off the chill. "What do you mean, worse?" she asked, her voice echoing slightly in the empty space.

Lucas turned towards her, his face pale in the moonlit gloom. "Elyria saw an opportunity—an opportunity to wield power, to dominate it. She promised a ritual to suppress the beast within, to control the wildness threatening Selene."

"And?" Grace's heart raced as she urged him to continue.

"It backfired," Lucas admitted, pain etching his features. "Instead of taming her, it unleashed her. Selene became wilder, more ferocious. She began attacking the townspeople, becoming the monster she most feared."

Grace felt a wave of anger and betrayal wash over her as the pieces fell into place. "Elyria lied to us," she said, her voice hardening with each word.

"Yes," Lucas agreed, his shoulders bowed as if carrying a great weight. "And when I confronted her, she claimed to have perfected the ritual. She convinced me to try again, this time with me. She played on my deepest fears, Grace—my fear of becoming like Selene."

Grace stepped closer, her eyes locked on his. "Lucas, I'm so sorry," she murmured, the distance between them closing in more ways than one.

Lucas shook his head, a wry smile flickering briefly. "Don't be. I should have seen through her. I should have protected Selene, protected all of us."

Silence enveloped them, heavy and contemplative, as they stood amidst the ruins of what was once a sanctuary. Grace reached out, her fingers gently brushing his arm. "We'll fix this, Lucas. Together."

Meeting her gaze, Lucas found a glimmer of hope amidst his guilt. Together, they stood in the heart of the den, a place of past horrors and present resolve, ready to face whatever lay ahead.

CHAPTER 16

The woods outside Redwater had always been a place of whispered stories—dark tales that parents used to scare their children into behaving. But now, those stories are becoming real. Too real.

Grace's heart thudded in her chest as she stepped into the clearing, the faint light of morning failing to dispel the dread hanging over the forest. The smell hit her first—sharp, metallic, the unmistakable scent of blood—and she had to swallow back the bile rising in her throat.

There, sprawled across the forest floor, was the body of Jenna Taylor. Her former tormentor. The one who had made Grace's life hell for years. The one whose cruel words and spiteful pranks had always felt like a weight, pulling her down, suffocating her.

Now, Jenna was the one who lay in the dirt, her body twisted and contorted in unnatural angles, her blonde hair matted with blood, her eyes wide open in a frozen scream. The violence was unfathomable. The wounds were deep, jagged—claw marks that tore through flesh and bone like a rabid beast had gone to work on her.

Grace took a shaky step forward, her breath caught in her throat as she recognized the markings. The gouges in the trees surrounding the body were unmistakable.

Claw marks. Those same claw marks that had haunted her nightmares, the signature of something far older, far darker, than anything they had ever known.

But they were from a wolf. Something worse stalked these words.

And it had taken the girl's tongue, leaving her mouth open, gaping and empty.

The realization sent a chill through her, crawling down her spine. Jenna Taylor, the girl who had tormented her every chance she got, who had humiliated her in front of the whole town... she was the latest victim. And yet, as much as Grace hated her, as much as she had wished for Jenna to finally suffer some kind of consequence for her cruelty, the sight of her lifeless body twisted with such brutality made Grace feel a sickening knot in her stomach.

It was the animals in the woods. They weren't just attacking at random anymore. They were growing bolder, more ruthless. And the truth sank in like a cold blade—they were coming closer.

The town had always dismissed the threats from the forest as nothing more than superstition. A part of her had thought the same thing, too. But now, staring at Jenna's mutilated body, there was no denying the truth: something terrible was out there. And it was hungry.

Grace's eyes moved over the scene, the blood, the savagery. She could feel the weight of the town's expectations bearing down on her. They trusted the Letteux family to protect them, to handle whatever horrors came from the forest. But she wasn't so sure they could anymore.

"They'll deal with it, right?" Grace asked, her voice barely a whisper.

Grace's throat tightened, but she couldn't pull her eyes away from the body of Jenna Taylor. It didn't matter that Jenna had tormented her. It didn't matter that she had spent years making Grace's life a nightmare. No one deserved this. No one deserved to die like this.

But the town had grown used to ignoring the creeping terror in the woods. They trusted the Letteux. They *had* to. But Grace wasn't so sure they could stop what was coming. The creatures—the monsters—were only getting stronger, and the Letteux family couldn't shield them forever. She could feel it in her bones: the darkness was closing in.

She turned back to the clearing, the sight of Jenna's body haunting her. The woods were no longer just an ancient mystery. They were a threat—a very real threat.

And they were coming.

The manor held its breath.

Dusk hadn't yet fully fallen, but the halls of the Lutteux estate were already thick with shadows—long, listening things that seemed to follow Grace as she padded barefoot across the cold stone floor. Her heart thudded in her chest like it wanted to warn her.

Lucas moved like smoke behind her. Silent. Watchful. Barely brushing the tapestries as they ducked through the side corridor that bypassed the grand hall. If anyone saw her sneaking a werewolf into the ancestral home, it wouldn't end in questions—it would end in blood.

They reached the west wing, long sealed and recently reoccupied.

Elyria's sanctuary.

The door was unlocked. Of course it was.

Inside, the old study had been transformed. The family's relics—once solemn and sealed behind glass—were now woven into arcane chaos. A blood-marked grimoire lay open beside a steaming bowl of herbs. The air smelled of rust and roses. Candles flickered beneath sigils chalked into the floorboards. The manor's ancestral calm had been corrupted into something more volatile. More *alive*.

Elyria stood at the far end, not surprised in the least. Her silhouette cut against the low fire like a shadow wearing skin.

"Grace," she said with a smile too serene for the hour. "And Lucas. How thrilling. Sneaking your monster in through the servant passages? Is this a secret rebellion, or just nostalgia?"

"Don't play games," Grace snapped, stepping forward, her voice sharp with nerves and fury. "You live in our house, eat from our table, and twist the magic you swore you abandoned. You said the ritual would help Selene. You made her worse."

Elyria closed her book with a soft, deliberate snap. "No, darling. I *revealed* what was already inside her. You all just preferred not to see it." Her gaze slid to Lucas, unreadable. "Some things must break before they can be healed."

Lucas moved forward, teeth bared beneath civility. "You experimented on her."

"And she survived," Elyria countered. "Which means she is strong. Which means *we* are close."

Grace clenched her fists. "You call that progress? You left her screaming at the moon."

Elyria walked toward them, slow and elegant. "I have refined the process. I believe it can stabilize her—perhaps even reverse the corruption. But I need your help, Grace. You're not just another Lutteux. You *are* the curse's heir. Isolde's blood sings through you, and that makes you the key."

Lucas stepped protectively in front of Grace, his presence a low, steady warning. "You've had your chance. You don't get another."

Elyria's eyes gleamed, amused. "That's not your decision to make, wolf."

Grace's body ached with the weight of the moment. She hated the way part of her wanted to believe Elyria. To *hope*. She hated that her hands—meant to wield blades—might be the ones needed to untangle this centuries-old nightmare.

Lucas's hand brushed hers, just briefly. Enough to ground her. Enough to say *I'm here*.

The silver bracelet on Grace's wrist thrummed like a warning—ancestral power fused with doubt. Blood remembering blood.

The fire in Elyria's chamber was already burning when they returned. Grace hesitated at the threshold—Lucas silent at her side—but Elyria merely looked up from her ink-dark scrolls, as if she'd been expecting them all along.

"You've come back," she said smoothly, rising. "Good."

"No more games," Grace said, stepping forward. "If you want us to trust you, then tell us *everything*."

Elyria's smile sharpened. "Then listen well."

She moved to the hearth, the shadows curling around her like robes. "Under the next blood moon, the curse will thin—its hold stretched taut. It's the only time I can anchor a ritual powerful enough to affect all of them at once. But I need every cursed soul gathered. *All* of them."

Lucas stiffened. "Even the corrupted?"

"Yes." Elyria turned, her eyes landing on him like a challenge. "Especially them. The curse festers in isolation. It must be drawn together to be reshaped."

A silence fell.

Lucas looked at Grace. She didn't flinch.

"The old refuge," she said softly. "The one past the Hollow. It's abandoned, but sacred ground. The curse *knows* that place. It'll listen there."

Lucas nodded, jaw tight. "I can get them there. Tomorrow night."

Elyria moved quickly after that, unrolling lists of ingredients, muttering names Grace didn't recognize. "I'll need wolfsbane, obsidian ash, powdered silver, thread soaked in lifeblood... And these."

She crossed the room and pulled three small jars from a locked cabinet, each one carefully wrapped in crimson cloth. They clinked faintly as she set them into a woven basket, and Grace could *feel* the weight of them, even through the silk. Each jar pulsed faintly with something not entirely physical. Like a heartbeat echoing in glass.

"What are they?" Grace asked, voice low.

"Anchors," Elyria said simply. "For the curse. Don't open them. Don't *look* too closely. Just get me what's on the list, and bring these with you when you return. We don't have long."

Grace stood in the witch's chamber, the basket heavy in her hands, the weight of a thousand lives humming in the jars beneath the cloth.

And the blood moon was already rising.

A soft knock echoed from somewhere deeper in the manor.

Voices. Stirring.

"Someone's awake," Grace whispered. "We have to go."

Elyria's smile didn't falter. "Then run. But come back when you're ready to *win*."

As Grace and Lucas slipped back into the shadows of the hall, her pulse pounded with fury, fear... and something else.

Not power.

Responsibility.

They slipped through the manor like shadows—silent, breathless, hearts thudding in sync. Grace didn't think, didn't plan. She only knew she needed to be far from Elyria's eyes, far from her father's judgment, from the history that burned in every room.

So she led him to hers.

Only once the door shut softly behind them did the realization hit her—*this is my bedroom.*

Her hand froze on the doorknob.

Lucas looked around, quiet but curious. His eyes swept over the space—not with derision, but intent. The walls were soft green, the wood dark and weathered, lined with old books, worn jackets, and half-polished blades. Her desk overflowed with notes and broken charms. A locket hung beside the window, catching moonlight like a secret waiting to be confessed.

She was suddenly, painfully aware of everything:
The pile of half-folded clothes slumped on her chair.
The pressed flowers curling in the corners of her mirror.
The faint, lived-in scent of herself that clung to the room.

And Lucas.

Lucas in her space.

A wolf in the heart of her sanctuary.

"I didn't mean—" she started, voice cracking, cheeks flushing hot enough to burn.

Lucas turned toward her — a slow, deliberate motion.

His eyes caught the spill of moonlight, bright and unreadable.

"It's... you," he said.

"What?" she whispered.

He took a step closer — deliberate, slow — and the air seemed to shrink around her.

"This room," he said.
 "It feels like you.
 Like something soft trying to hide inside steel."

She couldn't breathe.

Didn't know if she wanted to.

She dropped onto the edge of the bed to anchor herself — an instinct, a reflex.

And immediately regretted it.

The bed.

Her bed.

Not that kind of moment.

Not that kind of trust.

But still.

Still.

Lucas sat beside her without a word.

His shoulder brushed hers — casual, inevitable.

He was close enough that the heat of him soaked through her skin like wildfire.

Silence thickened.

Not awkward.

Not hesitant.

Charged.

Every breath scraped the air between them raw.

Grace turned toward him — drawn like a moth to a flame that would burn her clean.

And Lucas turned too — slow, inexorable.

Their faces so close she could feel his breath against her lips, uneven and warm.

Her dagger was across the room.

Her doubts somewhere far beyond that.

Only him.

Only this.

The kiss wasn't rushed.

It was slow — *deliberate* — like a question carved in teeth and breath and hesitation.

His mouth brushed hers — the barest, trembling whisper of a touch.

And when she didn't pull away —

When she leaned in instead —

Lucas made a low, rough sound in the back of his throat, like he was losing a fight with himself.

His hand cupped her jaw — careful, reverent — the thumb skimming the bruise at her jaw with a touch so light it made her whole body tremble.

Grace's fingers twisted in the fabric of his shirt — needing something to hold onto, something to fall against.

Her head tilted.

Her mouth parted.

The kiss deepened — not a collision, but a *surrender*.

Soft at first, tasting of winter and dark woods and something feral barely held in check.

Then deeper.

 Hungrier.

A slow devouring.

Grace's heart thundered against her ribs.

 Her body pressed against his like she could soak the danger out of him.

 Or sink into it.

He tasted like everything she wasn't supposed to want — frostbite and wildfire, blood and night.

And she wanted.

Oh, God, she *wanted*.

When they finally broke apart, their breath tangled between them.

Grace didn't let go.

Couldn't.

Neither did he.

He leaned his forehead against hers — a silent, desperate bridge between them.

"You don't scare me," Lucas whispered, voice raw.

"Not even with her blood in you."

Grace closed her eyes, her hand still pressed to the wild beat of his heart.

The air smelled of him now.

Her skin ached with it.

She exhaled — shaky, wrecked.

"You should," she whispered back, because it was the only truth she had left.

"You really, really should."

But she didn't move away.

And neither did he.

She exhaled slowly, her hand still resting over his heart.

And for the first time that night, Grace let herself *breathe*.

"You don't scare me, wolf-boy" and it was only half true.

He stayed.

Curled at the foot of her bed like some broken guardian, half-wolf, half-boy, all trouble. His fingers had found hers sometime after midnight, a quiet, accidental tangle between sleep and memory. And now they rested there—touching, not holding, like neither of them dared to call it what it was. Grace stared at the ceiling, heart thudding, skin burning with the echo of that kiss. The feel of his mouth still haunted her lips: wild and reverent, sharp as teeth, soft as breath. She shouldn't have kissed him. She shouldn't want to again. But gods, she *did*. And wasn't that the problem? That this boy—this monster—fit too easily into her room, her bed, her bloodstream. That she wasn't afraid of him at all.

CHAPTER 17

She hadn't meant to stare.

But there he was—*still here*—sprawled at the foot of her bed like the woods had followed her home. The early light painted his skin in muted gold, catching on the shadows of his lashes, the curve of his mouth, the collarbone just visible where his shirt had slipped loose in the night.

Grace's breath caught.

There was something impossibly still about him, even now. Like the forest was sleeping in his skin.

He stirred, and her eyes snapped up, too slow.

Lucas blinked blearily, turned his head, and met her gaze.

For a second, neither of them moved.

Then his lips curled into a slow, sleepy smirk.

"Were you watching me sleep?"

Grace flushed, instantly defensive. "You were drooling. I was making sure you didn't choke."

He laughed—low and rough and *unfairly attractive*—and then, somehow, they were both shifting at the same time. Moving closer without meaning to.

And then they kissed.

Easy. Familiar. Like they'd done it a hundred times.

It wasn't planned. It wasn't hungry. It just *was*.

But it ended too soon.

A breath. A blink. And it was over.

He pulled back first, just barely, forehead brushing hers. His eyes searched hers, and for a second, Grace almost reached for him again.

Almost.

She leaned back instead, clearing her throat, trying—and failing—to sound unimpressed.

"Still drooling, *wolf-boy*," she muttered.

Lucas grinned.

"You like it."

She did.

And that was the problem.

Lucas stepped back, already calculating. "I'll go summon them- my people- tonight. They'll need time to gather—and to trust me."

He turned toward Grace, his expression unreadable in the firelight. "You'll be safe here?"

"They are my family..."

He hesitated—then touched her wrist gently, just once, where her bracelet met skin.

Then he was gone.

The light scriff of Lucus's footsteps had just passed when Virgil confronted her in the hallway, his expression stern and uncompromising. She scanned his face but nothing suggested he'd nearly come face to face with a werewolf stalking his own halls. That a werewolf has spent all night in his sister's bed as they lay talking and cuddling.

"Grace, we need to talk," Virgil said, his voice low and foreboding. He gestured for her to follow him into the study, a room filled with old hunting trophies and the palpable weight of their family legacy.

Once inside, Virgil closed the door and turned to face her, his arms crossed. "I know you've been seeing Lucas and involving yourself with his kind more than is wise. It's compromising your judgment."

Grace's heart sank. She knew this confrontation was inevitable, but that didn't make it any easier. "Virgil, I'm trying to find a solution that doesn't just involve killing. There's more at stake here—"

"Enough, Grace!" Virgil interrupted, his frustration boiling over. "You're either with us or against us. Our family has hunted these creatures for generations. It's our duty to protect the town, and every moment you hesitate, you put us all at risk."

Grace felt the sting of his words, knowing how deeply her brother believed in their cause. "What are you asking me to do, Virgil?"

Virgil's eyes narrowed, his gaze piercing. "Prove where your loyalties lie. Help us hunt Selene. If you're truly a Lutteux, you'll put family and duty above all else."

The ultimatum hung in the air like a blade, ready to sever whatever remaining ties she had with her brother if she chose differently. Grace took a deep breath, her mind racing with the implications of her decision.

"Virgil, I am a Lutteux," she began slowly, her voice firm despite the tremor she felt inside. "But I believe there's a way to uphold our duty without needless slaughter. I want to save Selene, not destroy her. That's what our ancestors would have wanted—to end the curse, not perpetuate it."

Virgil shook his head, disappointment etched across his features. "You're naive, Grace. But I'll give you a chance to prove me wrong. Just remember, actions have consequences, and I will do what must be done, with or without you."

As Grace left the study, her resolve hardened. She knew the path she chose would be fraught with danger and might drive a wedge between her and her family, but it was a risk she was willing to take for the chance at a lasting peace.

After the confrontation with Virgil, Grace sought solace where she always did—in the vast, shadowy aisles of the family library. The rows of ancient tomes and the musty scent of old paper always had a way of calming her nerves. However, this morning, her search was not for peace but for answers.

She moved through the dimly lit shelves, her fingers tracing the spines of books that held secrets of centuries past. The Lutteux family library was a treasure trove of arcane knowledge, much of it gathered and preserved by generations of hunters before her. It was here, in the oppressive silence, that Grace stumbled upon an old leather-bound book tucked away in a forgotten corner. Its cover was dusty, but the emblem of a blood moon was still discernible, etched deeply into the material.

With a cautious reverence, Grace opened the ancient text. The pages were yellowed with age, but the writing was meticulously clear, penned with an elegance that spoke of a careful and learned hand. The book detailed the Blood Moon Prophecy, a legend she had heard whispers of but never fully understood.

As she read, the words seemed to leap from the pages: "When the blood moon rises high, and the shadows devour the light, a great sacrifice must be made to quell the darkness that stirs within the beast. Only then can the curse be broken, and peace restored."

Grace's heart raced as she absorbed the gravity of the prophecy. The term "great sacrifice" echoed ominously in her mind. She pondered its meaning—was it a sacrifice of life, or could it be something less literal, perhaps a sacrifice of one's own nature or destiny?

CHAPTER 18

In her dream, the forest around her was bathed in an eerie, blood-red light. The trees cast long, menacing shadows, and the air was thick with a foreboding silence. Grace walked through this dreamscape, her steps uncertain, her heart pounding in her chest.

As she moved deeper into the forest, a figure emerged from the shadows—a dark silhouette, indistinct yet imposing. The figure stood in the path of the blood moon's light, its features blurred but its presence undeniably powerful.

The shadowy figure whispered, its voice a chilling blend of echoes, as if speaking directly from the depths of the night. "The path of sacrifice is the only way," it said, the words swirling around Grace like a cold wind. "What you give will determine what you gain. The balance must be maintained."

Grace tried to speak, to ask what sacrifice was needed, but her voice caught in her throat. She felt an overwhelming sense of destiny enveloping her, the weight of her family's legacy and the curse they bore pressing down on her.

Suddenly, she awoke, gasping for air, the dream's intensity lingering like a shadow on her mind. The moon was still high, its light now a gentle silver rather than the ominous red of her vision. She rose, steadying herself against a tree, her mind racing.

The words of the shadowy figure echoed in her head, "What you give will determine what you gain." Grace understood then that the ritual might require more from her than she had anticipated. The notion of sacrifice hung heavily over her, a foretelling of the possible price to be paid for the curse's end.

With a renewed sense of urgency and resolve, Grace returned to the ritual site. The dream had not weakened her; rather, it had fortified her determination to see this through, whatever the cost. As she rejoined Lucas, Elyria, and the others, her face was set, her eyes clear. The time to act was now, guided not only by the wisdom of her ancestors but also by the dark prophecy revealed in her vision.

The courtyard was nearly empty when Emily found her.

Grace stood alone beneath the bare branches of the hawthorn tree, her arms crossed tightly against the chill that had little to do with the night air.

"Grace," Emily called, her voice soft but urgent.

Grace turned, the moonlight casting her face in sharp, uncertain angles. For a moment, neither of them spoke.

Then Emily crossed the distance between them and pressed something small into Grace's hand.

A pendant—a rough scrap of old silver, misshapen and battered, threaded onto a thin leather cord. The kind of thing a child might wear for luck.

Grace curled her fingers around it.

"I found it in my mother's things," Emily said, voice shaking. "It's nothing special. But it's been lucky for a long time."

Grace swallowed, the words thick in her throat.

"I'm coming back," she said.

Emily shook her head, a shaky smile pulling at her mouth. "Promise me anyway."

Grace hesitated.

She thought about the ritual. About Lucas, and Selene, and the creeping pull of blood and fate.

Still, she looped the leather cord around her neck, tucking the pendant beneath her shirt where it rested against her heartbeat.

"I promise."

Emily let out a breath that was almost a sob.

Then, because they were still them, she bumped Grace's shoulder with her own, the way they always had when things felt too big to name.

"You're the stupidest brave person I know," Emily muttered.

Grace smiled—small, cracked, but real.

"I learned from the best," she said.

And when she walked away into the shadows, the pendant was a warm, steady weight against her chest.

Night fell like a blade.

The forest was hushed under the rise of the blood moon—massive and wrong, swollen red like an open wound in the sky. It bled its light over the clearing, turning the trees to bones, the faces of those gathered to masks of shadow and suspicion.

Hunters lined one edge of the ritual circle, hands tight on silvered weapons. Lucas's pack stood opposite, eyes flickering, jaws tight. Between them stood Grace—silver charm bracelet burning cold on her wrist, heartbeat louder than the chants rising in the trees.

"This ends tonight," she called out. "Not with steel. Not with teeth. With choice."

A few hunters looked away. One werewolf spat on the ground. But no one moved.

Lucas stood rigid, arms crossed tight over his chest, muscles straining like he barely held himself together.

His eyes flicked from the hunters sharpening silvered blades to the wolves shifting uneasily at the edges of the clearing.

Nobody trusted each other.

Nobody trusted this.

His jaw flexed hard enough Grace could see it from where she stood.

"Grace," he muttered — so low it barely rose above the sigh of the wind.

"We shouldn't be here."

She turned toward him.

And her heart almost shattered.

Because the fear in his voice wasn't for himself.
It was for all of them.
It was for *her*.

"We don't have another choice," she whispered back, throat raw.

"If there was any other way—"
Her voice cracked.
"I'd take it.
But this... this could *free you*."

Her words hung between them, heavy as blood.

"All of you."

Lucas shook his head slowly, as if trying to loosen the terrible weight pressing down on him.

His brow furrowed — not in anger.

In *dread*.

"We don't even know what she's really doing," he said, voice fraying apart.

"She's twisted the truth before.

What if this isn't salvation?

What if it's just control?"

Grace stepped closer before she could think.

She took his hand — his real hand, not the clawed half-wolf thing he tried so hard to bury.

His skin was hot and shaking under hers.

Not from weakness.

From restraint.

She squeezed tight, feeling the tremor run through his bones.

"I trust you," she said — not a prayer, not a plea.

A promise.

"And I need you to trust me.

Just once more."

Lucas stared at her.

And in that single, frozen heartbeat, Grace saw everything:

The fear he didn't want to show.

The wild, desperate need he couldn't kill.

The hope clawing at his ribs, furious and fragile.

He looked at her like she was a cliff edge —

The leap and the fall both.

"For Selene?" he asked, voice scraping low and broken.

Grace swallowed against the thick knot of grief in her chest.

"For Selene," she said.

"For you."

Her thumb brushed against the back of his hand — a tremor of tenderness neither of them could afford.

Lucas closed his eyes for a long, battered second.

When he opened them, there was no more doubt.

Only terrible, trembling trust.

He nodded.

"Then let's do this."

They stepped forward together, hands clasped — hearts hammering wildly in their chests, pounding not in unison but in some ragged, desperate rhythm that was theirs alone.

The circle swallowed them — hunters and wolves watching with sharp eyes, suspicion burning from every corner.

Elyria raised her arms.

The chanting began — low, rhythmic, rising.

The world tilted.

The ground shuddered.

Grace never let go of Lucas's hand.
Not even when the magic snapped around them like a noose.

Not even when the air grew too thick to breathe.

Not even when she felt the terrible truth between their joined palms:

If this fails, it will break him.

And she will have to find a way to survive the wreckage he leaves behind.

But still —

She held on.

Because she couldn't remember anymore if she was saving him.

Or if he was saving her.

Elyria stood at the center of the circle, draped in blood-red robes, her arms spread wide as she began the chant. Her voice wove through the air like smoke, smooth and sinuous, ancient syllables slipping from her mouth like something remembered too late.

Grace's eyes were drawn to the basket beside her aunt—those *jars*, still wrapped in silk.

Something was wrong.

Then Elyria began.

She opened the first jar. A *tongue*, slick and pale, fell into her palm like meat at a butcher's altar.

Jenna.

"Last a tongue that wronged our blood."

The words hit Grace like a slap.

"No," she whispered, too softly.

The second jar opened. Two severed hands, pale as wax, wedding ring still clinging to bone.

The land developer.

"A hand that struck the blood."

The third jar—*a lump,* unformed and slick, slid free into the circle. A brain.

The man who attacked Virgil.

"A mind that plotted against us."

Grace's knees buckled. "You used the murders—*you caused them.*"

Elyria looked up. Her smile was soft. Serene. *Inevitable.*

"I corrected what was broken."

The ritual surged.

Lucus screamed, sharp and unholy and almost yanking his hand from hers.. Around them, the wolves cried out as power twisted through them like a blade through silk.

Mist rose from the ground—*not white but silver*, rippling with scent and magic and something older than curse.

The chanting coiled around them like smoke.

Lucas gripped her hand — not gently.
 Tight.
 White-knuckled.

Like if he let go, he would shatter.

Grace squeezed back, grounding him — grounding herself — their palms slick with shared fear.

"Stay with me," she whispered.

"I'm trying," he rasped, voice shaking.

The mist stirred, thickening, slithering toward their boots like fingers seeking flesh.

The wolves stiffened.

Low whines and growls started to rise from the circle.

And then it hit.

The wolves convulsed first — bodies writhing, gasping.

Bone cracked.

Limbs twisted.

Flesh reshaped.

Grace turned sharply — heart hammering — but she never let go of Lucas's hand.

Until he did.

It happened fast — and horribly slow.

The mist clawed up his legs, swallowing his boots, then his knees.

Lucas staggered — pulled away from her by a force she couldn't fight.

His fingers wrenched from hers — not by choice.

By violence.

"Lucas—!"

She reached out blindly — too slow.

He tried to move — tried to reach her —
but his body buckled, twisting.

"GRACE—!"

His scream tore through her like a blade.

And then he collapsed.

Right there beside her — one heartbeat he was standing, breathing, *hers* —

The next, he was on the ground — gasping, shrinking, convulsing — the mist devouring him.

The wolves howled — a chorus of pain that curdled the blood in Grace's veins.

One by one, their bodies diminished —

becoming small, frail, wrong.

Grace dropped to her knees without thinking.

Her dagger clattered from her belt, forgotten.

All she saw was Lucas.

He was curled on his side —

fur sleek and limp —

body too small, too still.

She grabbed for him — pulled him against her chest.

"Come on, Lucas, come on, stay with me—"

But he didn't move.

He didn't breathe.

"No," she choked out.

"No—no, please—"

She buried her face in his scruff — breathing in the scent of ash, of him, of loss —

and sobbed so hard her body shook.

Around her, the hunters began regrouping — cold, efficient, voices sharp.

The wolves staggered, dazed, smaller, wounded.

But Grace didn't hear them.

Couldn't.

She cradled Lucas's broken body against hers — rocking slightly — pressing her mouth against his fur like she could kiss life back into him.

"I'm sorry," she whispered against him.

"I'm so sorry. I never meant—"

Her words dissolved into gasps.

She hadn't freed him.

She had destroyed him.

Elyria screamed. "This isn't what I cast! *This isn't what I bound!*"

The magic had turned on her. The curse had twisted again.

The mist rolled in low and thick over the training grounds, creeping like a living thing across the stones and the roots. Grace turned, heart lodging in her throat, just as the little pug staggered into the clearing, tail wagging lazily.

The mist wrapped around it, clinging and pulling, soaking into the folds of its squat body until the shape beneath began to ripple and swell. Bones cracked, skin stretched, and the pug's form twisted, grotesque and fluid, reshaping itself.

Hunters cried out as the creature grew—first the size of a wolf, then larger still, until it stood nearly the size of a pony, muscled and hunched, its fur smoking with residual mist.

Its body resembled something lionesque—broad-shouldered and heavy, with thick limbs ending in razored claws. The once-familiar jowled face now stretched and split into a monstrous grin, teeth too many, too long.

It let out a wet, hacking snort—half laugh, half cough—and shook the last tatters of mist from its mane.

The nearest hunters screamed and fell back, weapons raised, faces pale with horror. Someone dropped a sword with a clatter.

The beast only chortled—an ugly, guttural sound—and loped forward with an almost lazy arrogance, tail flicking behind it like a whip.

It wasn't attacking.

It was *parading*.

Like it knew there was nothing they could do.

Grace stood frozen, breath tearing in and out of her lungs, as the creature passed her with a rolling gait, its heavy paw brushing the dirt like a king surveying his broken court.

The mist clung faintly in its wake, cold as frost, and carrying the sharp, metallic scent of old silver—*and something rotting underneath.*

With one last look—full of nothing and everything—it loped into the unhappy dark.

The clearing erupted in confusion. Hunters drew weapons. Wolves crouched, whimpering, unsure. Elyria staggered back from the circle, hands coated in blood and betrayal.

Elyria backed into the trees, face a mask of fury and wonder.

"You broke it," she whispered to Grace. "You *broke* it."

And then she vanished into the forest after her creature.

CHAPTER 19

The silence after the mist cleared was not relief.

It was horror.

Dozens of wolves crouched in the clearing, breathing hard—smaller, softer, stripped of the power that once made them fearsome. Fur still bristled over clawed limbs, but there was something stunted in them now. Not human. Not whole. Not free.

The first cry came from the hunters.

Then another. Then—

"We end it now."

"Finish them before they shift again!"

"They're weak—this is our chance!"

Thomas stepped forward, silver axe in hand. His eyes burned. "It's mercy. Better now than later."

And Virgil—

Virgil didn't hesitate.

He stepped beside his father, sword drawn, his face hard and unflinching. "They're still cursed. You saw it. This isn't salvation—it's a stall. We wipe it clean. All of it."

Lucas lay crumpled against Grace's chest, no heavier than a child in her arms.

His breath ghosted faintly against her skin — shallow, broken.

Alive.

But only just.

Grace rocked him gently, trying to breathe through the sobs still racking her.

Her hand cradled his skull — feeling the small, fragile bones there — terrified that if she let go, he would slip away for good.

The clearing was chaos around them — wolves whimpering, hunters regrouping.

And then—

The heavy, deliberate crunch of boots on frosted earth.

Grace looked up, heart plunging.

Virgil.

His sword gleamed silver-bright in the moonlight, the blade still slick from the rites they had sworn to obey.

He moved without hesitation, without mercy — his eyes dead, his body all cold, rigid violence.

Not her brother.

Not now.

Just a hunter.

Just an executioner.

"Move," Virgil barked, voice flat.

Grace's breath caught.

She clutched Lucas tighter.

Virgil advanced — sword rising.

Grace's own blade lay somewhere in the mud — *forgotten, useless.*

There was no time.

No weapon.

No choice.

Only **her.**

Without thinking — without a breath of hesitation — Grace **threw herself over Lucas**, shielding his limp, broken body with her own.

The world cracked.

Virgil's sword froze mid-swing — just above her spine.

Time held its breath.

Grace braced herself for the pain.

For the betrayal.

For the end.

Her arms tightened around Lucas's small body, tucking his head against her heart.

She would not let them take him.

Not like this.

Not after everything.

Not after he had trusted her.

If they wanted to kill him—

If they wanted to finish what the ritual had started—

They would have to kill her first.

The fire snapped wildly behind her, the only sound in the frozen clearing.

Grace waited.

And waited.

Her heartbeat pounded against Lucas's fur — frantic, human, real.

Then—

The tension broke.

The whistle of a blade lowered — sharp, furious.

Bootsteps retreating, hard and fast, cutting away into the dark.

Virgil.

Cursing.

Spitting.

Walking away.

Grace didn't lift her head right away.

She stayed huddled over Lucas, trembling, breathless — a living shield.

Only when she felt Lucas shift weakly under her — a broken, breathy whine catching in his throat — did she finally dare to move.

She peeled herself off him slowly — careful, shaking — her hands gentle as prayer.

His green eyes fluttered open — glazed, dazed, *but there.*

Alive.

"Lucas," she gasped, voice wrecked.

His small, battered body pressed instinctively closer to her.

Around them, the hunters watched.

Judging.

Waiting.

But Grace no longer cared.

She had made her choice — bloody and irrevocable.

And she would live with it.

Or die with it.

Lucas looked up at Grace, his eyes still his own—but trapped in a body not meant to hold him.

"I'm so sorry," she whispered, collapsing beside him, wrapping her arms around the now-smaller wolf. "I didn't know. I didn't *know*..."

She blinked up at Lucas, her eyes momentarily clear—and then they flickered, a low growl curling from her throat. Her mouth opened, not in words, but in teeth. The curse was still there. Subdued, but lurking. *Waiting.*

"She stole it. None of them are better" Grace said, the words catching in her throat like ash. "None of them are cured. The curse... it just changed."

Lucas let out a low, broken whine. Grace dropped to her knees beside him, arms around his diminished frame.

"No," she said, her voice sharp with grief and fury. "They are *not* beasts to be culled."

Virgil's expression twisted. "You'd protect *that* over your own family?"

"I *am* protecting my family," she snapped. "And you'd murder them for not being perfect? For not healing the way *you* wanted?"

"They'll turn," he growled. "They always do."

"Then we stand guard. We *watch*. We will try *again*."

The hunters surged, some yelling, some readying blades. Chaos rippled at the edges of the circle like fire waiting for dry brush.

Then Marielle stepped between them.

Her voice rang out like a bell in a warzone.

"*Enough.*"

All heads turned.

She moved toward the center, hands raised, face like carved stone. "You want to slaughter children in the name of control? You want to finish what Elyria started? Then you've already lost."

Thomas faltered. Virgil's jaw clenched.

"They are weakened, yes," she continued. "But they are still *our responsibility*. Our duty."

Virgil didn't answer.

Marielle's voice softened—but it cut deeper. "You're angry. We all are. But this is not the moment to fall to fear. This is when we *choose* who we are."

She turned, met every hunter's eyes.

"Stand down."

The clearing froze.

One by one, weapons lowered. Blades sheathed. Breath held.

Virgil was the last. For a heartbeat, Grace thought he might strike.

But then his grip loosened, and he turned away.

"This isn't over," he said.

"No," Grace whispered, holding Lucas close. "It's just beginning."

The manor had never felt so empty.

Not even in winter, when the wind howled through the broken eaves.

Not even after her mother's silences, brittle as frost, or her father's rages that shook the walls like earthquakes.

No.

Tonight, the silence felt different.

Heavier.

Suffocating.

As if the house itself was grieving.

Grace shoved the door to her room open with her shoulder, clutching Lucas tighter to her chest.

He didn't resist.
Just curled in smaller, tighter — a trembling weight no heavier than a bundle of broken twigs.

He hadn't spoken since the ritual.
Had barely even whined.

Only tried — and failed — to shift back.
Over and over, until his tiny body shook and he finally collapsed into a shivering sleep.

The fire still guttered in the grate, casting thin, sickly gold across the room.

It touched the edges of her cluttered desk, the silver charms on the windowsill, the worn quilt folded neatly at the foot of the bed.

All the familiar things — the ordinary, innocent things — now looked like relics.
Artifacts of a life she no longer lived.

Grace lowered Lucas carefully onto the bed.

He whimpered, soft and hoarse, but didn't stir — just curled tighter, tail tucking under his small, battered body, nose pressed into the pillow.

Her pillow.

The sight of it — of *him* — cracked something deep and awful inside her.

She sank onto the edge of the mattress, staring at him.

So small.

So broken.

So **wrong.**

The fire snapped hollowly in the silence.

Grace buried her face in her hands.

"I'm sorry," she whispered — voice barely human.

"I thought... I thought I was saving you.

I thought I was strong enough."

Her words dissolved into nothing.

What did apologies matter now?

What could she say to a boy whose body she had offered up to the ruin she'd called "hope"?

Tears stung behind her eyes, then blurred her vision, spilling down unchecked.

She pressed one hand into his fur — clutching at the last pieces of the boy he used to be — the boy who had once held her hand with strength and certainty and fierce, foolish trust.

Her own body felt alien now.

Heavy.

Too heavy.

Too human.

She hated the blood that sang so thick and hot in her veins while Lucas lay cold and wasted beside her.

Why did she get to survive?

Why did she get to stay whole while he was carved down to this?

The betrayal of it was a knife twisting under her ribs.

Her breath came in gasps now, wracking sobs she couldn't silence.

She curled beside him — tucking her legs under herself, pressing her face against the rise and fall of his side.

His fur smelled like earth and ash.
 Like something scorched but *still alive*.

Still him.

God, still him.

Her tears soaked into his coat.

The fire dimmed to a guttering whisper.

Her silver bracelet pulsed faintly at her wrist — a heartbeat, a warning, a wound.

It felt too tight.

Too heavy.

Another chain she couldn't break.

"I swear," she breathed against his warmth, "I swear I'll fix this."

Her voice cracked on the words.

"Even if it kills me.

Even if it means following her into hell."

She laid her hand carefully over his small chest — feeling the slow, stubborn beat of his heart against her palm.

The only proof he was still with her.

The only thing she hadn't lost.

Not yet.

"You saved me," she whispered.

"More times than I can ever count."

Her throat closed around the last words.

"Let me save you now."

The room blurred into darkness.

The fire stuttered.

The cold crept in.

But still she stayed.

Curled around what was left of him.

Cradling the broken pieces like a prayer.

The forest was different in her dream.

The trees stood tall, but there was no whisper of hunger in their branches. The moon hung gentle and gold above, casting light without weight. Grace stood on a hill where no blood had been spilled, her silver bracelet glowing softly at her wrist. Below, wolves ran—not hunted, not cursed—but free. Among them, she saw Lucas, unshackled, unbroken.

And then he turned, human and whole, smiling at her in a way he never could in waking life.

She took his hand.

When she woke, her fingers were curled around the bedsheet, not his, but her heart still beat with the rhythm of *possibility*.

Grace found her mother in the greenhouse, tending moonbloom with shaking hands. The glass walls bled with dew and silver light. Marielle didn't look up as Grace approached—just said, "She's still out there."

Grace nodded. "We need to find her."

Marielle paused, breath catching. Then, softly: "Bloodroot runs deeper than bloodlines. I studied it once. Before I was your mother. Before the family bound me in oaths." She touched the soil, fingers sinking into it like memory. "If she used true magic to vanish, I can feel the thread. *Track* it."

Grace's throat tightened. "Can you undo what she did to Lucas?"

"I can try." A pause. "But I can't protect you from what comes next."

"I don't need protection," Grace said. "I need the truth."

The dream came on silent feet.

No mist.

No howling.

Only the cold, soft hush of a world stripped bare.

Grace stood in the center of a dead forest.

The trees were skeletal — gnarled fingers clawing at a starless sky.

The earth was ash beneath her boots — dry, crumbling.

And everywhere she looked, there were wolves.

They circled her — dozens, maybe hundreds — their bodies hunched and thin, their eyes hollow lamps of devotion.

Not alive.

Not dead.

Something in between.

They bowed low to her.

Pressing their snouts into the ash.

Trembling with reverence.

As if she was a goddess.

As if she was a curse.

Grace looked down at her hands.

Not hers.

Too pale.

Too sharp.

Her fingers shimmered with silver lines — markings, bindings — the same sigils Elyria wore carved into her flesh.

The silver bracelet on her wrist was gone.

In its place, chains of delicate bone wound up her arms, rattling when she moved.

The wolves whimpered at her feet.

Waiting.

Wanting.

For a command.

For a kill.

For *worship*.

At her back, the graves stretched on and on — shallow pits clawed into the ash, scattered with shattered bones.

So many.

Too many.

In the center of the graveyard —

One grave deeper than the rest.

One marker darker.

Older.

Grace stumbled toward it, heart pounding.

She fell to her knees beside it.

The name carved into the stone blurred and twisted under her fingers — but somehow, she still saw it.

Still *knew*.

Lucas.

She opened her mouth to scream — to deny — to undo — but the wolves howled in unison, drowning her out.

Their bodies pressed closer — suffocating her with their heat, their need, their hunger.

Not for freedom.

Not for salvation.

For her.

Only her.

Grace staggered back — hands clawing at her arms, the chains rattling louder.

She tore at her skin — trying to rip the silvered marks free — but they only sank deeper, inked into her bones.

She looked up — and across the graveyard, framed in the dead trees, stood Elyria.

Smiling.

Proud.

Triumphant.

Grace tried to run —but her feet stayed rooted.

Heavy.

Bound.

The wolves pressed closer — their fur brushing her legs, their teeth bared in twisted worship.

And somewhere inside her chest, something dark and wrong and *aching* whispered:

This is what you were always meant to become.

The dream cracked.

Splintered.

Grace fell into blackness—

—and woke gasping.

Sweat slicked her skin.
 Her bracelet burned against her wrist, hot and heavy.

The fire had died in the grate.

Lucas stirred in his sleep beside her — a soft, broken sound that anchored her, that reminded her he was still there.

Still breathing.

Still hers.

But the dream lingered.

And in the hollow behind her ribs, fear bloomed anew.

Not fear of losing him.

Not fear of dying.

Fear of what she might become if she couldn't save him in time.

One full cycle.

One brutal, endless turning of the sky.

Grace had counted every night by the brittle beat of her heart.

By the way her silver bracelet pulsed cold against her skin.

By the way Lucas's absence hollowed out the world.

She had watched the moon crawl across the heavens — wax, wane, die and be born again.

And all the while, Lucas remained trapped.

Small. Silent.

A wolf's shape.

A man's soul blinking out behind bright green eyes.

Until tonight.

Tonight, the moon rose clean and full — no blood, no ritual-stained red.

The Hollow exhaled under the white light, cleaner and quieter, as if mourning and mercy had finally found a balance.

And Grace found him there — where the old stones leaned drunkenly at the edge of the trees.

He leaned against the broken archway, head bowed, arms folded tightly across his chest.

Still.

Tense.

Almost afraid to move.

Human.

Painfully, heartbreakingly human.

Her breath caught.

Her boots crunched over frost-tinged leaves as she approached — slow, hesitant, half-convinced he would vanish if she blinked too hard.

When Lucas looked up—

When his green eyes found hers—

She didn't see the wolf.

But she didn't see the boy she remembered either.

There was something wild lingering in him now — something shattered and stitched imperfectly back together.

He was human.

But not whole.

Not really.

He smiled — slow, tired, crooked — but when she stepped closer, he stiffened.

Almost flinched.

As if her touch might unravel him again.

Grace reached out with trembling hands.

She touched his chest — felt the erratic thrum of his heartbeat under her palm.

Not steady.

Not strong.

But real.

Alive.

Tears burned behind her eyes.

"We're not done," she said, voice breaking under the weight of everything they had survived, everything they had lost.

Lucas covered her hand with his own.

Rough.

Warm.

Shaking slightly — a tremor he didn't seem to notice or couldn't stop.

"We're just getting started," he said, voice hoarse, not with certainty, but with brutal, desperate hope.

He leaned in — slow, hesitant — like a man stepping onto thin ice.

His forehead brushed hers.

Grace tilted her head up, breathing him in — fire, cold, sorrow.

When she kissed him — it wasn't slow.

It wasn't clean.

It was ragged.

Hungry.

His mouth found hers like he was afraid this would be the last time.
 Like he was anchoring himself to her before the world shattered again.

Her fingers tangled in the fabric of his shirt — yanking him closer.
 His hand slid into her hair — but he hesitated — shaking — as if he thought touching her too hard might snap the fragile thing he had become.

He kissed her like he was drowning.

And she kissed him back like she had already decided to go down with him.

There was no world.

No curse.

No broken bloodlines.

Only the terrible, beautiful, fragile thing that pulsed between them.

When they finally tore apart — breathless, foreheads pressed together — Grace kept her eyes squeezed shut.

Because she was terrified that if she looked —
he would be gone.

Lucas's smile faded — not in fear, but in grim, shuddering understanding.

"I can only shift back," he said, his voice rasping against her skin, "on the full moon."

Grace's heart twisted in her chest.

"I know," she whispered.

And she meant it.

She meant it with her whole blood-soaked, broken body.

"I don't care."

The other nights —
　The long cold spaces between full moons —
　　He would remain caged.

Smaller.
　Weaker.

A man wearing a wolf's skin.

But he would still be him.

Still burning with the fierce, wild heartbeat of the Hollow.

Still the boy who had chosen her when he should have run.

She leaned her forehead harder against his.

Their hands tangled together — fingers knotting like lifelines.

The stars blinked overhead — soft, cold, patient.

Witnesses.

"We'll find a way," she whispered.

"Even if it takes a lifetime."

Lucas's hand tightened on hers — tight enough to hurt.

"Even if it kills me," he said.

And they stood there —

Not whole.

Not healed.

Not safe.

But still together.

Still fighting.

Still *theirs*.

Dawn came red and slow across the sky, casting long shadows over the manor gates. Grace stood dressed in leathers, her silver dagger sheathed at her hip, the charm bracelet glinting like a vow. Beside her, Lucas waited—his eyes sharp, his body tense, already halfway to wolf but still hers.

Marielle handed Grace a small satchel. Inside: herbs, ashes, and a glass vial glowing faintly with moonlight. "Follow the thread," she said. "And be careful, Grace. She's not the woman you remember."

"No," Grace said. "She's something older."

Lucas opened the gate.

Together, they stepped onto the path that led beyond the Hollow, beyond the edge of everything they'd known.

And far away, beneath roots and ruin, Elyria opened her eyes.

She smiled.

"**Let her come,**" she whispered into the dark.

"**I'm waiting.**" **Her creature laughed.**

The story continues in Book 2:

The Silver Betrayal

Book 2: The Silver Betrayal

Chapter One – The Quiet Between Howls

The forest had grown quieter since the curse broke wrong.

Grace used to hear the wolves singing at night, low and mournful—beautiful in their pain. Now there was only silence, like the woods were holding their breath. Like even the trees knew something had gone horribly wrong.

Lucas trotted beside her, small and limping, his coat too clean for a creature of the wild. He didn't howl anymore. Couldn't. His throat worked sometimes, like he was trying, but no sound came out—only breath. Ragged. Silent. Rebellious.

She hated the way people looked at him now. Like he was a pet.

They'd passed through two towns already. She'd told them he was a mutt. They'd believed her. But sometimes the children stared too long. One old man had crossed himself when Lucas growled.

Grace didn't correct them.

She didn't have the strength.

The road wound through black pines, the kind that didn't whisper. The kind that watched. Grace kept her hand near the hilt of her silver dagger, though she hadn't drawn it since the night the ritual shattered.

That night still lived behind her eyes. Elyria's laughter. The wolves screamed as their bones bent inward. Lucas's hand slipping from hers as fur overtook it.

And the worst part—Grace had let it happen. She had asked Elyria for help. She had *trusted* her.

She wouldn't make that mistake again.

Lucas bumped her leg gently with his shoulder. When she glanced down, he was looking up at her, ears forward. Questioning.

"I'm fine," she lied.

His tail didn't wag. It never did anymore.

They reached the edge of a shallow valley by dusk, and Grace unfolded the cracked map Elyria had left behind—unintentionally or on purpose, she couldn't be sure. One corner was burnt. The path west led to a region she only knew by name: **The Hollow March**. Old witch territory. Forgotten magic. The kind that didn't want to stay buried.

Lucas nosed the edge of the paper. She watched his paw press into the dirt beside it, almost like he meant to point.

"West," she whispered. "You think she's there."

He didn't nod—he never could. But he looked west and didn't blink.

Grace folded the map, tucked it back into her coat, and straightened. She was tired. Of running. Of failing. Of breaking things she loved in the name of saving them.

But she had made a promise.

I'll fix this. I swear it.

And this time, she wouldn't break it.

She took the first step down the ridge. Lucas followed, silent as shadow. Together, they walked into the dusk, toward a curse that had learned to run—and a love that refused to die.

The wind shifted.

Lucas froze.

Low in the valley, something was howling. But it wasn't a wolf.

It was laughing.

Printed in Great Britain
by Amazon